Morwen Cottage

LEANN L. MORGAN

authorHOUSE

AuthorHouse™
1663 Liberty Drive
Bloomington, IN 47403
www.authorhouse.com
Phone: 1 (800) 839-8640

© 2018 LeAnn L. Morgan. All rights reserved.

No part of this book may be reproduced, stored in a retrieval system, or transmitted by any means without the written permission of the author.

Published by AuthorHouse 12/23/2017

ISBN: 978-1-5462-2164-7 (sc)
ISBN: 978-1-5462-2162-3 (hc)
ISBN: 978-1-5462-2163-0 (e)

Library of Congress Control Number: 2017919286

Print information available on the last page.

Any people depicted in stock imagery provided by Thinkstock are models, and such images are being used for illustrative purposes only. Certain stock imagery © Thinkstock.

This book is printed on acid-free paper.

Because of the dynamic nature of the Internet, any web addresses or links contained in this book may have changed since publication and may no longer be valid. The views expressed in this work are solely those of the author and do not necessarily reflect the views of the publisher, and the publisher hereby disclaims any responsibility for them.

To Dacey's Cornish Tours
David Warner and Harold Holman

&

Tour Cornwall
Tim Uff
Your hospitality will never be forgotten

Acknowledgments

I'd like to thank Science Fiction, Romance author *C.A. Jamison*. Besides being a gifted author, she did a wonderful job of editing and proofreading for me. In moments when my writing became grueling, her encouragement kept me moving forward. Plus, she gave me good tips on how to write romance.

I also thank *Jane Easterly* for her professional proofreading and input on my story. I value her opinion. She introduced me to the NaNoWriMo challenge and this manuscript is the result of it.

And to my beta readers, *Dan Murphy, Gayle Gerard, Tom Reagor,* and *Pepper Bauer,* thank you for taking the time to read and critique my story. You helped me tremendously.

To *James Clark,* a good storyteller and *Seth Morgan,* a writer; two of the sweetest grandpas a girl could ever want.

And thank you, *Phil Gerard,* for being my best friend.

Chapter One

Gravitation is not responsible
For people falling in love.
(Albert Einstein)

Rowena threw the envelope with her divorce papers into the fire. She tossed in her ex-husband's clothes. She feverishly looked at the rest of the contents lying on the ground, his electric razor, his raunchy magazines and his favorite comb, the color of his thick dark hair still clinging to the teeth. She grabbed them all and tossed, the pages turning brown then curling up into ashes, his comb melting into an odd configuration.

Rowena looked around her backyard where she stood. Where there once had been a beautiful wildflower garden, now remained only dried stalks and weeds. A hummingbird flitted around the area in search of something to nourish from, found nothing and flew away.

The whole lawn needed mowing, but the lawn mower no longer ran, the spark plug lying worthless on top. She snatched it and threw the plug into the fire with such force the flames spit upwards. *Good riddance.*

Rowena bent down and picked up the box with all his love letters and poems. She considered for a moment before ripping at them, one by one, tossing all the lies, promises and broken dreams into her private inferno celebration.

Rowena's neighbor, Terri, stood watching from across the street. She called over. "Are you alright?"

"Just doing a little house cleaning is all. My divorce went through this morning."

"In that case let me get some wine." Terri walked back to her house.

Terri had always been there for Rowena, her home at times a refuge.

"Thanks, Terri." The two of them held up their glasses. "Here's to no more living with a hedonistic serial cheater."

"And here's to no more gas-lighting from your mother-in-law." They clicked their glasses together in a toast.

"Can you believe it's been four months since he walked out? By the way, you can call me Miss Mills now; I took back my maiden name."

"Now that is something to celebrate." Terri pitched her wine glass into the fire.

Rowena, her energy spent, threw hers in too.

"I am worried about you. You have lost weight almost to the point of emaciation."

"Yes, the great divorce diet."

After Terri left, Rowena went back into the house. The space seemed empty, desolate. The plaster on the walls needed repair, but there was not enough money to fix them. The roof needed replacement, resulting in a large water stain on the living room ceiling.

She went upstairs into the bathroom, and then looked up at herself in the mirror. She was startled at the ugly scowl staring back at her in the reflection. Her once attractive heart-shaped face had turned gaunt with no softness in her hazel green eyes.

She made herself smile and applied some clear gloss to her bow-shaped lips, then playfully made a pout. Rowena released the stretchy band holding her hair and ran a brush through her long wavy locks. She softened her eyes and wiped a smudge spot from her cheek. With a glance into the mirror, she said, "I vow to never scowl again."

It didn't matter that she was having an extended nonproductive spell as a writer and living in a rundown house that stood almost in foreclosure. Each issue had to be dealt with one at a time. The whole healing process would be slow. She would have to fight to get to her better self. She must reinvent herself. Still, she was liberated.

In the kitchen, days of neglected mail littered the table. Among the pile a certified notice drew her attention. With the letter causing her adrenaline to pump a little, she hopped in the car and headed straight to the post office.

The postmaster shuffled through some letters and found Rowena's. The postmark said Great Britain.

"Great Britain? Who do I know from there," she whispered to herself as she sat in her car opening the letter. It stated a woman named Maude Hollister, her father's aunt, left her entire estate in Cornwall, England, called Morwen Cottage, to Rowena. The letter came from a lawyer named Peter Chapman whose office resided in Morcant Cornwall. She got on her phone and googled Morcant. It was a small village near the Bodmin Moors.

As Rowena tried soaking all of this in, she glanced up and out of nowhere appeared William, her ex-husband, walking on the sidewalk right by her car with the new love of his life, holding hands. The woman stood tall and voluptuous with long, dark hair, and luminous blue eyes. Rowena sighed and leaned her head back against the head rest. She knew of three things she could never give William: blue eyes, raven hair and big kahunas.

Chapter Two

As Rowena found her seat on the flight out of St. Louis that warm September evening, she wondered if she had made the right decision auctioning off her home and furnishings to pay off her debts, leaving her with a mere twenty thousand dollars. The only tangible things she had left were in her two suitcases.

She rested her head back on the seat, and her mind drifted back to that night thirteen years ago when she met William Dryer.

She had just broken up with her high school sweetheart, Daniel. Going off to separate colleges, they'd drifted apart. Or Rowena had drifted anyway. Daniel had pleaded with her to please give their relationship another try, but she had her mind made up. Daniel was blond and stocky and had the nature of being kind, decent and predictable.

Daniel was every mother's dream for their daughters. But starting her freshman year and only eighteen years old, Rowena wanted to spread her wings. She cared about him deeply but not in the way of romantic commitment. With a profound sense of guilt and a sentiment of great sadness, she broke it off with him.

Rowena's friend Pamela had given a Christmas party for her friends returning home from college. She could still sense the cold winter night with the smell of pine filling the air and how the Christmas lights sparkled in Pamela's home.

"It's strange to see you here without Daniel." Pamela placed a gift under the tree. Pamela had a gift for everyone. She was so thoughtful that way.

"You're not complaining because I broke up with him?" Rowena rubbed the pulsing vein by her left temple. "Mom beat you to the punch, and I don't want to hear it again."

Pam tossed her hands in the air. "Not me." She drew a line across her mouth. "Nope, my lips are sealed."

Rowena went over to sit by the tree. She dearly loved Christmas time. Sitting there with the glow of the lights it seemed so atmospheric and romantic. And for a brief moment, a tinge of sadness enveloped her.

Pamela handed Rowena a glass of champagne.

Rowena raised her glass in a toast of freedom and over the tiny bubbles her eyes locked on to a flawless silhouette. The most beautiful man she had ever laid eyes on, chiseled-jaw handsome.

Well, maybe a little short and wiry. His front teeth slightly bucked. But his face seemed perfect, almost too perfect for a man.

"Who's the hottie?" Rowena grabbed her friend's arm. "Don't turn around. He's staring straight at me." Rowena took a sip and tried to look away. "He's the guy with all the drooling girls standing by him."

"Oh, you must be talking about William Dryer. He's friends with my brother John." Pamela smiled. "Yes, he is quite the Romeo. I think he just broke up with his girlfriend."

Rowena looked up at him. She couldn't take her eyes off of him. He looked her way and their eyes locked for a moment. He smiled, and it sent a shock wave down her spine. She self-consciously cast her eyes down, embarrassed she was caught staring.

He approached Rowena and her heart started racing.

"You have pretty eyes. The sort of color you can't quite name," he said very casually as he sat down next to her.

She had never thought of her eyes as pretty before or anything else about herself for that matter, but standing there in the warmth of his aura, her desire grew.

"Hi, my name is William. May I ask your name?"

His eyes stunned her, they were dark and intense. She observed his straight Roman nose. "My name is Rowena. Thank you for the compliment." She wanted to say more, something intelligent but her mind turned into mush.

"Would it be too forward to ask for your phone number? I would like to get to know you better." He winked.

Rowena looked up to see a couple of girls nearby staring at her with peeved expressions on their faces. The pulsing started again at her temple. She wanted to say yes in the worst way. But she had just pledged freedom. "It appears you could have enough phone numbers without adding mine to your collection." She smiled and darted her eyes in the direction of the two girls. "Thanks for asking but I think I will pass for now." She excused herself and got up to find Pamela.

Later that evening as Rowena was leaving to go home Pamela stopped her and gently pulled her aside. She whispered, "Daniel has given you consistency and loyalty when you have been a bit inconsistent. William is the type who will give you inconsistency when you need consistency the most."

Rowena shot Pamela a funny look. "Pamela, I didn't give him my phone number."

Pamela looked at her sideways as if to only half believe the innocence behind her statement. "Okay, I'm sorry Rowena, I promised to keep my mouth shut. You owe me one, but I care about you as a good friend and don't want you to get hurt."

Home in bed after the party, she couldn't stop thinking about William. She knew he wouldn't give her a serious thought. And more importantly she knew deep in her heart if he did give her a thought, it could lead to a treacherous relationship.

The next morning when Rowena went to get in her car, a note from William was on her windshield.

"Hello, Rowena.

I just wanted to tell you how glad I am to have met you. If you would just give me a chance, I would like very much to go out with you. You have me intrigued.

William."

Rowena looked up to see William parked across the street. She smiled.

Rowena went out with William for the rest of the Christmas break. Her mother Ingrid and grandpa Liam did not like William, sensing from the moment they met him that Rowena's best interest was not in his mind.

Her desire to become a writer had her studying English Literature her sophomore year. Although she lived five hours away, she and William communicated almost daily. She had fallen in love with him. He professed his love to her and Rowena wanted to believe it.

Eleven months later, on the night before Thanksgiving, Rowena caught a ride home with a friend. She dropped her things off at her grandpa's house, where Rowena and her mother lived. Her friend then drove her over to William's place and dropped her off.

Rowena walked up the stairs to his apartment. She knocked on the door and noticed a very dim light shining through the crack at the bottom of the door. With hesitation, William spoke from the other side of the door asking who was there.

"It's me, William, I came home early." Rowena knocked again. He didn't open the door. "William, please open the door, I am freezing out here."

"Now is not a good time, I think you better go home. I will come to see you later," he whispered sheepishly.

Rowena started pounding on the door and demanding to enter.

He opened up the door only wearing his jeans.

She started storming through the apartment when William grabbed her arm. With her heart pounding, she jerked away. She ran into the bedroom, and there was a woman.

Rowena stood there paralyzed, too shocked to cry. His ex-girlfriend Martha lay naked in his bed. A sheet covered her in an attempt to hide that fact. William had claimed the affair had ended.

Rowena left. She walked back the six blocks to her mom and grandpa's house in a daze. Her vapored breath from the cold silently disappeared and reappeared with each exhale; she shivered from the cold but more from nerves.

Rowena vaguely noticed lights on in the passing homes and wondered how life could go on as normal around her. She thought her life had stopped, or was she just floating in a nightmare ready to wake up any moment? If it was real, one could not hurt so profoundly and live on.

As Rowena walked in the front door her mother and her grandpa Liam were in the living room. She went through the motions of small talk with them, trying to act casually, not wanting to upset the holiday.

What Rowena really wanted to do was kick, scream and cry. Then have her mother take her in her arms, stroke her hair and tell her everything would be alright. But instead, she quietly went to her bedroom.

Rowena sat on her bed in the semi-darkness and stared at the gift she had purchased for William. Hanging over the door, the old leather bomber jacket was still in good shape. A real one she by chance had found at a thrift store. Something he had always wanted. She stood up and went to the coat, grabbing it off the hanger, throwing it in a dark corner of her closet.

The tears then started to flow, very bitter tears. Rowena went to grab a tissue from her vanity and noticed her prescription medication for menstrual cramps. She didn't really want to die, but she wanted the pain to die. A pain she had never felt before.

A realization came to her at that moment how much pain she must have caused Daniel. She picked up the phone to call him. As the phone rang, anxiety welled up in her until he picked up.

"Hi Daniel, it's me, Rowena, I thought I would call and see how you are doing."

There was silence for a long period.

Finally, he answered in a hesitant voice, one without any warmth or feeling, "I'm doing great, Rowena. Actually, I have recently become engaged."

Had her guilty conscience, mixed with anguish, played tricks on her, or had she detected a slight bit of glee in his voice?

Rowena mustered up every ounce of strength left in her, "I'm very happy for you. Your fiancée is a very fortunate woman. I am so sorry if I hurt you," she said with a throat that was tight and constricted. It hurt to talk anymore.

"No harm done. Have a good life, Rowena. Goodbye."

She tried to say good bye, but her words were strangled. She gently laid the phone back on the cradle.

She sat on the bed again; this time tears of real sorrow flooded out and down her face. With grief combined with self-pity, she picked up the bottle of medicine. She knew she should call a friend, anyone, to help with this pain, but she didn't want to disturb anyone's holiday.

In a moment of complete illogical contemplation, she opened up the bottle and put six pills in the palm of her hand. She looked in the mirror and loathed what she saw. In a flash, she put the pills in her mouth and swallowed them all at once with a gulp of water. She gently laid the bottle back on the vanity.

Chapter Three

"Grandpa, if you don't mind, I am going to borrow your van to visit with some friends." Liam's pride and joy was a 1962 vintage Volkswagen van he kept as an extra vehicle when needed.

"Sure," he said distracted. His response mixed with the games blaring on the TV, as Rowena slipped past.

She got into the van and backed out of the driveway without a thought to where she was going. She just kept driving until she got to the edge of town. Rowena then turned left onto a remote highway.

The sign ahead read 16 miles to Mapletown.

Right outside of town she slowed down at the Catholic graveyard. In the strange ambiance of the dark moonless night, the area oddly seemed comforting. Among the plotted ground her beloved Grandma Ilsa was buried in the second row.

She turned off her turn signal when a dark figure appeared in front of her van's lights. He waved his thumb over the road. In the remoteness of this highway, the long-haired guy would most likely have a hard time finding anyone to pick him up.

Light headed and muddled, she pulled the van over to give this person a ride.

Rowena rolled down the passenger window. "Where are you going to?"

He leaned down and peered into the van. "Up the road to Mapletown, but my feet are killing me, and I'd really appreciate a lift."

Rowena invited him into the van, and they continued down the highway. When they were about halfway there, the medication started to kick in.

She pulled over. "I'm feeling awful right now, could you drive the rest of the way, please?" Her nausea took hold.

Rowena staggered out of the car, held the hood as she walked around and plopped into the passenger seat.

He climbed into the driver's side and turned to Rowena. "Are you alright?" he asked. The concern in his voice seemed genuine.

And she answered in a quiet, breathy voice, "I took some medication earlier that has made me feel very queasy. I'm sure it will pass."

He pulled out and proceeded to drive on until they finally came to the house where the guy lived.

So caught up in her own sorrow and sickness, she didn't bother to ask his name or why he had been hitchhiking. As she got out of the van and back into the driver's seat, her sickness overcame her again. She knew she couldn't drive back home.

She staggered out of the van to get some fresh air. All at once the medicine hit like a ton of bricks, and she fell to her knees and started to vomit. She tried to stand, but the world became a spinning carnival ride. She went to her knees again.

This time the man held her hair back as she vomited again and again. "I think you better come inside the house to lie down, or maybe you need to go to the hospital." The fear in his voice worried Rowena.

"No, I will be alright." She sighed. The strength in her voice, body, and mind had all but faded.

He then took her arm and led her towards his front door. "Have you overdosed?" He narrowed his gaze.

With a jumbled mind, she followed him into the house. "I took some prescribed medication on an empty stomach. It'll pass." Her awareness numb from weakness, she surrendered to his offer of lying down on his bed.

The nice young hitchhiker turned down the sheet and helped her get in. "Rest for now. Thanks for saving my feet." He turned the lights down low, put a glass of water by the bed and let her alone.

She dozed off for a while. When she awoke, a dark sky blocked the view through the window.

Searching for a clock on the night stand, she knocked over the glass of water. "Oh, crap."

He came into the room. "How are you doing?"

"I'm doing much better. I really must be heading back now. Please get a towel so I can mop up the mess I made." As she stood up she staggered a little.

"I think I better drive you back, you still don't look very well." He ran to get a towel and dabbed at the water spill.

So in the deep of the night, this complete stranger got into her vehicle and quietly drove her back to the point where she had picked him up earlier by the graveyard.

As he stepped out of the van he asked, "Are you sure you are going to be alright?"

"Yes, I will be fine. But I hate that I put you through this drama."

"My feet feel better. I can handle the walk now."

Without either one asking each other's name or anything of substantial meaning, the man started walking back to Mapletown in the darkness.

Chapter Four

Rowena sat in the van trying to clear her head a bit. Again nausea overcame her. She grabbed the van's trash bag; a relic to go with the van. It had a hole in the back that slid through a knob on the dashboard. She heaved into it.

Rowena stepped out of the van still holding the bag and shaky from weakness, slowly walked into the graveyard.

She found her grandmother's grave and fell onto the cold wet grass, now dry heaving and spitting into the bag. The wet grass cooled her heated body, and it strangely comforted her. In her drug addled state, she fell into a deep sleep.

She woke up at the beginning of dawn shivering, the dampness penetrating through her coat down to her skin. She slowly got up to walk, stumbling at first back to the van, throwing the plastic bag into a receptacle.

She tiptoed into the house without disturbing anyone. She went into her room and peeled off her damp clothes, then slipped on a nightgown and crawled into the warm bed. The softness of the bed engulfed her like angel wings even as her head throbbed from dehydration.

With her hands trembling, she took the water glass from the night stand and took a small sip, gagging slightly. Before drifting off to sleep, she thought about the hitchhiker. Anything could have happened, he could have killed her. But he helped her. Somehow she would thank him.

Just as she relaxed her aching muscles and drifted into a deep sleep, her mother came into her room and asked that she help with the Thanksgiving preparations.

Rowena forced her feet onto the floor and moved her weary body into the bathroom. Exhausted, she washed her face in cold water and searched for the zipper on her house coat. She yanked the tiny, metal part up and headed toward the kitchen.

As her mother basted the turkey, she asked, "How did last night go with your friends?

"I didn't tell you last night I went to see William and he had another woman at his place," she tried to explain without drama, "so I doubt if he will be here today." She wanted to tell her mother everything but was afraid to; ashamed to. What she had done was the epitome of any mother's fear.

For a moment her mother lost focus on their conversation as Rowena's petite Aunt Agnes came into the kitchen and went to greet and hug her. She then gave Rowena a robust hug and her new breast enhancement smashed up against Rowena.

"What is this I just overheard about that pip squeak of a man called William?" Aunt Agnes bolstered. She batted her eyes, thick with liner and glitter, at the two women.

Agnes, boisterous and gregarious always had her emotions on the cuff of her sleeve and all over the place. She had a sarcastic, dry sense of humor but could also be very soulful, sweet and gentle. A brunette with dark eyes by nature, her long hair was bleached platinum blonde and pulled to one side into a ponytail.

"Rowena went over to William's apartment last night and caught him with another woman. I honestly don't know what she sees in the guy. I knew the moment I met him with those shifty eyes, he would be nothing but trouble. She deserves so much more and would be so much better off without him. It's like he has a spell on her." Even when perturbed, Ingrid spoke in a soft voice.

"Uh hello, I'm here in the room thank you very much." Rowena had to smile. She always smiled whenever Agnes was in the room.

"Trust me, Rowena." Aunt Agnes cleared her throat. Her husky voice chatted with reminders of days when she smoked and drank whiskey. "No man is worth losing your health over. Honey, you look pale. Find a good man; someone like your father. One who will walk a thousand miles barefoot on a path with broken glass and swim the length of the Mississippi River with only a snorkel and a wind breaker. I have always said if a man doesn't act like you are the center of the universe he isn't worth having."

"That's so true Rowena, listen to your auntie," Ingrid interjected. "For heaven's sake, don't swim the deep-sea for someone who wouldn't jump a mud puddle for you."

"And if he plays that hard-to-get bull shit, over and over again, he doesn't really want you; he is addicted to an adrenaline rush. You don't want that. Forget about those damn smoothies who are in constant need to have their pathetic egos stroked. They will tell you what you want to hear, just to get what they want, blowing smoke up your wazoo. Move on darling." It was full steam ahead for Aunt Agnes.

Ingrid smiled. "Preach it, sister."

Rowena thought to herself about Agnes, "Well, you maybe didn't **always** say that." She remembered a story told about her. How could anyone forget?

Agnes had become engaged to a guy of questionable scruples. Against her parents' wishes, they ran off to get married. But it turned out there was this little bit of a problem—he was already married with a family.

When it finally all came to light about him, Agnes abruptly quit her job and turned up missing, leaving no word to her where-a-bouts.

Everyone went into a complete panic. The authorities suspected her lover of foul play which most likely delighted Agnes.

They finally found her sitting on a rocky beach in San Diego sipping a margarita. Her only comment, "I have just committed suicide to my epic tale of a past life."

Rowena wanted to tell Agnes everything. Everything. She would have understood. She would have scolded her, admonished her, and told her she put her life in great danger, but she would have listened. She just couldn't bring herself to do it. Maybe someday she would tell her, but not now.

Rowena understood their concerns. "I know you both are right—" when her grandpa entered the kitchen.

"Does anyone know what happened to the trash bag I keep in the car?"

Chapter Five

The Thanksgiving meal that day included Ingrid, Aunt Agnes, Uncle Robert and Grandpa.

After Aunt Agnes recovered from her fiasco in San Diego, she came back to live in Illinois. She met and married Robert Trueheart. And his heart proved to be as true as his name. The polar opposite of Agnes, he was quiet and reserved and maintained an even disposition.

Agnes asked Ingrid, "How are your headaches?"

"They come and go. The doctor put me on a new medicine. It seems to help a little."

Rowena worried about her mother's head pains, and she knew stress made them worse, another reason to watch what she told her.

"I hope this medicine kicks in and does the trick, Mom. They have some—"

There was a knock at the door—it drew the attention away from Rowena. "Excuse me." She dabbed her lips with a napkin and left the table.

Rowena put her eye to the peephole. William. She opened the door, and he stuck a bouquet of sickly roses in her face. She lowered her chin and opened the door wider to allow him passage. A rose bud fell from the stem as she took the flowers and let them hang upside down from her hand. He obviously had found someplace open that had their old wilted flowers on clearance.

She wanted to slam the door in his face, but her head was pounding so badly there was no strength to fight. She gave the door a swift swing to let it slam behind him. Without a word, Rowena dropped the flowers in the trash can next to Grandpa's chair.

William entered the dining room and Liam and Robert, not yet knowing what had transpired between William and Rowena greeted him, and told him to grab a plate. Ingrid looked perturbed. He sat down between Agnes and Rowena.

Aunt Agnes leaned toward William. "What in the hell are you doing here?" She whispered. "Rowena told me all about what happened last night."

"Last night was a great misunderstanding." He drew his eyebrows together, and his face blushed scarlet.

Agnes glared at him until he was forced to look at her. "You may think you have everyone else fooled, but I know your type. If you ever hurt my niece, you will have to answer to me."

Robert's jaw dropped, and his mouth hung open. He tapped her lightly on the arm and discreetly put his index finger to his mouth to shush her.

William whispered back, "I adore Rowena and plan to make it up to her for the rest of my life."

"Don't even go there with me." Agnes had fury in her eyes. Robert tightened his hand a little on Agnes' arm. She jerked her arm out of his grip.

William looked at Rowena with passion in his eyes. He smiled and winked at her. He gets close to her ear and whispered. "I love you."

No one else, thank heavens, noticed how she could hardly eat. Not even William. He should have noticed.

After the meal, they went to sit in the family room where William pleaded with Rowena to forgive him. His eyes gleamed with moisture. The sadness on his face fooled her. He cried.

"Could you possibly forgive me? I love you, Rowena, I really do, let's get married. I can't stand the thought of being without you. I have made a terrible mistake. In a moment of weakness, I allowed her to seduce me. You are the only one for me. Even last night I could only think of you. I promise to never do anything like this again." He lowered his gaze.

She sat there for a long time silent, weak, only breathing. Only breathing. That's all she had the strength to do. Every promise, he'd ever spoke, came with the word I. Never once were the words we, together or happy, uttered from his mouth.

But without an ounce of ecstatic euphoria and a sense of pending doom, she foolishly and mindlessly surrendered to his pleading and reluctantly said yes. A marriage proposal, swimming in doubt and then drowning as William sucked all of the air out of the room. Why couldn't she just have taken her mother and Agnes's advice?

She broke the news to her mother and grandpa Liam. Back in his younger years, Liam would have jerked William out of the house and continued kicking him on down the street. But he had mellowed with age.

So without much thought, planning or incident, they were married. Aunt Agnes loaned Rowena her wedding dress. As her mother helped place the veil on her head, she took a look in the mirror at her ivory completion and forced a smile.

Rowena dropped out of her sophomore year, mid-term. She went to live at Williams's apartment. She found a job at the local newspaper, doing advertising at first, and then writing a weekly column. It honed her skills enough where she started writing on her own and even started making some money at it. She had hoped one day to write a novel.

William started at a local car manufacturing plant right out of high school, working his way up to department manager. Credit did *have to be given to William for being a hard worker, and he worked well with others.*

One day Rowena drove over to Mapletown to try and find that mysterious man who had helped her. She had guessed he was a college student at the University by the general location of the house, but couldn't figure out the exact place.

She had it embedded in her mind what his face looked like, surrounded by long, curly light brown hair. And he was quite tall and thin.

She believed she had found the home once, but going to the door to enquire, nobody of that description lived there.

"What would you like to drink with your meal?" The flight attendant asked. Rowena opened her eyes.

"Water will be fine, thank you."

Rowena only picked at her food. The man next to her started snoring after he finished eating. She closed her eyes again, recalling her sorted memories, shaking her head.

It really wasn't so much about William and how he behaved but what it said about her. What a gullible fool she had been. How could her self-esteem have been so stamped out as to allow something like that to even transpire?

There are facets of a man that capture your romantic dreams

while you are dating them, even a man who is your direct opposite. But after you marry, these opposite attractive traits will no longer be appealing if they are not in your core values. And your romantic passion will especially die if your mate is unfaithful, no matter how much you pretend forgiveness.

Rowena had to admit, William excited her. She even had to admit she wouldn't have married him if he didn't have at least some redeeming qualities. And there were moments when he surprised her with a sweet and tender side.

A lot of William's essential beliefs came from a narcissist mother, a complaining badger to everybody and a punitive, unfit mother to her three children. She was a drunk and a druggie who in her addled mind, confused fact from fiction, causing grief to many. A single mother in desperation, she'd desert her kids for months at a time to satisfy her lust for other men.

Rowena had compassion for William's sad childhood but she didn't have the strength or desire anymore to help him with his broken wing. She needed to fix her own. Her life had changed colors.

Chapter Six

Yesterday's history
Tomorrow's a mystery
So live for today.
(Carroll Shelby)

Upon her arrival at Heathrow Airport, she rented a car for the more than four hour journey south-west into Cornwall. A lawyer by the name of Peter Chapman would be expecting her in Morcant, a small and picturesque village, about thirty minutes from the northern Atlantic coast.

The lawyer's office stood on a very narrow street with cobblestone sidewalks on either side. She found a spot to park and walked a block to the office, turning her head around admiring the quaintness of the place. With what little space between the sidewalk and buildings, a variety of lush flowers grew everywhere.

It appeared that most of the structures had living quarters on the second story above the businesses.

Floret pots hung with glorious mums by the curtained windows. The surrounding blossoms of sweet alyssum, gardenias and jasmine had such a magnificent fragrance she could smell them from the street. She spotted the entrance door to the lawyer's office which read: Peter Chapman, Attorney at Law. On each side of the exterior door two large pots had beautiful green ginger lilies in them. She entered the door which had a low casing.

Rowena walked inside. As soon as the lawyer spotted her, he hurried to toss a candy wrapper in the trash and stood up from his desk and walked over to greet her. She noticed he wore wing tip shoes. His paunchy physique appeared as though he'd spent too many hours behind his desk.

"Hello, you must be Rowena Mills." He brushed crumbs from his fingers and extended his right hand. "It's nice to meet you. I'm Peter Chapman. I've been expecting you. The legal documents are on my desk. Let me grab them." He returned to his workspace and rustled a few papers.

"Thank you. I have to say this village is wonderful, so quaint and lovely." Rowena looked around his office and even admired the paint on the walls. The center cream molding divided two different shades of brown and a palm tree in the corner gave the office a tropical appeal.

Peter sat down at his mahogany desk. "Please have a seat." He gestured to a plush brown leather chair. He handed her the legal documents.

Rowena looked them over. "I'm still in shock that this generous woman left her estate to me." She looked through the documents, becoming more astonished with each sentence. "And she has also left me 10,000 British Pounds?" She looked up wide-eyed.

He peered over his wire-rimmed glasses. "No finer woman lived than Maude Hollister."

"I sure wish I knew why she left the estate solely to me. Dr. Maude Hollister was my dad's aunt. I know my dad had a sister too. I don't know if she is still alive but she married and had a son."

Peter's eyes shifted back and forth. He changed the subject. "Maude's house has not been lived in for over three years. The estate is about five miles inland from here and in the moors. It's a historical home called Morwen Cottage."

"I have to admit I'm anxious to see the place." Rowena smiled.

"As you probably already know, Maude Hollister was one of the local general practitioners. Her health started to fail, but refusing to completely give up her practice, she welcomed a new doctor named Harry Reader to help share in her practice. Dr. Reader was born and raised in Birmingham and received his medical education in Edinburgh. Currently, he's the only doctor in Morcant."

"I vaguely remember my mom telling me my dad's aunt paid for his graduate school, and his sister Constance was jealous over

Maude's generous offer. I never did know anything more about that story." Rowena shrugged her shoulders upward.

Still evading her hints, Peter pushed up his glasses and continued. "She drove her car every Monday through Friday into the village from her home, which I have already stated is situated in the Bodmin Moors. Their local surgery is right across the street from my office." He walked over to the window to point it out.

Rowena stood up to look outside.

"One day Maude didn't show up at the surgery. Dr. Reader drove to her home and when he couldn't get any response, broke a window to unlock the door. He found her up in her bed, resting there peacefully; she had passed away during the night in her sleep. She died at the ripe old age of eighty-eight."

Peter walked Rowena to the door, "Your aunt was a very kind and considerate person. We all miss her very much. She became widowed at a young age and had no children, so the village was her family."

Rowena turned around. "I truly wish I could've met her."

"Dr. Hollister dedicated her whole life to the people of this village. Many times in the night she would drive into town to care for a sick child or sit for hours waiting for a baby to be born. I'm not surprised about Maude helping your dad with his college finances. Money didn't matter to her, unless she could help someone. Everyone treasured Maude, yes."

It heightened her spirits greatly to have Mr. Chapman express such kind words about her great-aunt. This time Rowena extended her hand. "Thank you so much. I'm sure we'll keep in touch."

Rowena walked across the street to the surgery and glanced in the window. Right above the window a sign read 'Harry Reader M.D. – General Practice'. She could see a reception nurse sitting at the front desk and several people sitting in the waiting room. She looked up at the second story and saw two windows dressed with curtains and wondered if Dr. Reader may live up there.

She walked into the entrance door of the surgery that led right into the waiting room. There were eight chairs with five of them being occupied. All of the walls were painted butter yellow, the floor a polished dark wood. The reception nurse looked up for a brief moment at Rowena as she talked on the phone. She held up her index finger to indicate she would be right with her.

Rowena looked up on a wall and noticed a picture of a woman and wondered if it could be her aunt, realizing she had never even seen a picture of her. The lady in the picture looked to be about sixty years of age. A bit on the plain side, having steely gray hair pulled into a bun and drab looking clothes. She appeared to be rather stout. Still, observing her eyes there was gentleness to them and a compassionate intensity that transcended even in the picture.

The woman hung up the phone and asked, "Hello, may I help you?"

She walked over to the desk and introduced herself. "Hello, I'm

Rowena Mills. I just arrived here in Morcant and wanted to see for myself the surgery that once belonged to my great Aunt Maude."

The fortyish petite receptionist with short salt and pepper hair looked very surprised and walked around her desk to introduce herself.

"You're her niece?" She extended her hand. "My name is Donna."

"I assume this is a picture of my great-aunt. Believe it or not, I've never seen or met her before. She looks to be very kind." Rowena pointed to the photograph on the wall.

"Yes, that's Dr. Maude. Oh— she was a lovely woman. I noticed straight up your eyes resemble hers."

Warmness welled up inside of Rowena to hear kind words spoken about her aunt again by another. "That's very kind of you to say."

Donna smiled. "Dr. Reader is busy at the moment; I know he would be very pleased to meet you. Won't you please have a seat?"

"Thank you, but I'll be here in the area for a while, so I promise to come back and meet the doctor. I'm quite anxious to see my aunt's estate." Rowena walked toward the front door, and then turned around. "Please, have a wonderful day."

Donna replied, "Of course, how lovely to meet you. I'll tell the doctor you were in."

Rowena got into her car and sat, musing; remembering the last day with her father. The images of her five year old childhood taunted her mind...

"No!" Mommy screamed.

A car jumped the curb.

Rowena's mother picked her up and threw her out of the way.

"You hurt me, mommy," Rowena screamed.

Her mother fell and hit her head.

Rowena heard the red car make a screeching noise on the sidewalk.

Her daddy's body laid twisted in a strange way. His eyes open, staring at the sky.

Her mother lay on the concrete, sleeping.

"Mommy, Daddy, wake up!" Rowena cried.

Her mother acted funny at the hospital. She threw up. She cried for daddy. "Stephen!"

Rowena covered her ears.

Her mother's head hurt, really bad. She cried a lot and couldn't stop.

"I hate red cars." Rowena thought to herself.

Rowena and her mother went to live with Grandma Ilsa and Grandpa Liam.

Chapter Seven

Driving into the countryside of Cornwall on the narrow winding roads, Rowena entered into some moorland. She couldn't take her eyes off the scenery replete with rolling hills, hedge fences and grazing sheep. The ancient stone barns stood picturesque with their sodded moss rooftops.

Rowena turned off onto a heathland area and followed a narrow lane becoming surrounded with the landscape of shrubbery and beautiful purple and yellow flowers; off into the distance she saw a group of Dartmoor ponies peacefully grazing. On the approach to the house, was an old wooden frame with a sign reading 'Morwen Cottage'.

To the left of the lane her deceased aunt's cottage came into view, surrounded by an archaic wooden fence and in bad need of paint. The Gothic house had lancet windows but so overcome with vegetation it was hardly visible. Out of the moss covered roof, with cedar shingles were two brick chimneys with battlements. The front yard had two huge gnarled oak trees. The scene reminded her of a Thomas Kincaid painting, only tired and sad without the illumination.

On the right of the lane, about 300 feet away she noticed a small chalet with smoke coming from the chimney.

She stepped out of the car and followed the barely visible flagstone walkway. On the covered wooden front porch, dried leaves crackled beneath her feet. Cobwebs draped over the window sills. The broken glass remained on the porch by the window where Dr. Reader had entered.`

Rowena unlocked the front door with an old ornate skeleton key. Slowly opening the arched entrance door, she spotted a fireplace in the front room and sagging floor boards which creaked as she crept across them. She walked through the kitchen and saw the second hearth. She attempted to open the back door, but couldn't get the wooden portal to budge because bramble had overgrown all around the cracks to the point of sealing it tight.

When Rowena went back outside to gather her luggage, the lushness of the air made her inhale deeply. Scanning the area, she could see for miles all around and it fascinated her. Brushing up against one side of the house stood a lovely white rose bush, robust, refusing to give in to the neglect. She became aware of to the silence in the air, hearing only the sound of an occasional bird tweeting or a sheep in the far distance, peaceful.

Rowena reentered the house and ascended the groaning, dust ridden wooden stairs. The place smelled musty and closed in. She took her luggage to a bedroom facing the back of the house, wondering if this could be the room where her aunt died. The two windows squeaked as she opened them to help air out the area.

Entering into the upstairs lavatory, the cast-iron claw-foot bathtub had a water pump for a nozzle. The vintage sink was the kind with separate hot and cold faucets and a drain plug connected to a chain.

Pumping the squeaky spigot connected to the tub, thick slushy rust came out of it. She heard a shutter outside hitting up against the side of the house where the nails had come loose on the boards.

Rowena did not know what to make of this place as she walked down the creaking floors of the upstairs hallway, but hoped a ghost or hobgoblin wouldn't make an unexpected appearance.

Back in the bedroom, she pulled out some bedding from an antique chest of drawers. Dust flew everywhere as she fluffed out the sheets and blankets on the bed. The house had a chill to it. Even after she closed the windows back up, the grubby and ragged curtains breathed in and out from a draft by the cracks. Peering outside, she saw a wood pile in the backyard, and would later have to gather some wood to light the fireplace.

But for the time being, she walked downstairs into the kitchen and sat down at the sooty, oak table. As she he scanned the room, her eyes stopped at a wooden hutch and then moved to where two of her aunt's coats and hats still hung on a hook by the fireplace.

What a humble and simple life my great-aunt lived in this house.

And without much appetite, Rowena opened up the bag from the market and ate a little bit of fruit.

Chapter Eight

While outside gathering wood, an elderly man approached Rowena. His body slight, he walked slow and hunched over. Approaching from where the sun set, his long silver hair glistened, like a cloud with a silver lining.

"Hello, young lady. You must be Maude's niece. My name is Manchester McGreevy." He extended his hand. "I live in the chalet across the lane."

She extended her hand back. "Hello to you. It's nice to meet you and so good to see someone out here. I was beginning to think I'd driven into some sort of serene no man's land. My name is Rowena Mills." Deep careworn wrinkles surrounded his brown clouded eyes. But they were sweet and welcoming. She liked his Cornish accent.

"It can be rather quiet out here, yes. Still, there's nowhere else in the world I'd rather live. By the way, I've just fixed up some autumn stew. Would you like a bowl?" he asked eagerly.

For the first time in months, her stomach growled with a voracious hunger. "Oh, that would be wonderful." She took the gathered wood to the porch and then followed Mr. McGreevy over to his home.

The front door led immediately into a small living room. There to greet them was a nice looking but aging chocolate Labrador dog with gray whiskers on his face. The pooch trotted around on the old wooden plank floors. The plastered green walls had many photographed pictures.

Rowena noticed one picture in particular on a shelf. A younger Mr. McGreevy, and by him sat a pretty lady with long, dark curly hair.

Against one wall stood a bookshelf filled with books, many of them classics: Hemingway, Fitzgerald, Jane Austin, Shakespeare and Mark Twain to name a few.

Rowena lightly ran her index finger along the row of books. "I'm from the area close to where Huck Finn and Tom Sawyer had their adventures."

"Really— you don't say?" He sounded curious. Mark Twain is one of my favorite authors. It's indeed a small world that we live in. Have you ever been to the Mark Twain cave?"

"I sure have. It's a show cave and quite spectacular."

"I've seen pictures; most beautiful it is, yes. In my younger years, I'd of loved to have visited there." Mr. McGreevy's eyes became animated. "Oh dear—where're my manners? Please, have a seat." The elderly man offered and gestured to a faded floral velvet sofa, worn with a shiny patina. A handmade croqueted doily lay across the back of it.

As Rowena sat down, the springs scraped a bit. An orange tabby lay opposite her on the cushion, sleeping.

Mr. McGreevy took ahold of both the arm rests of the matching chair and eased himself down.

The room filled with the wonderful scent of something delicious brewing, mixed with burning wood. The place most certainly had the touch of a female but it appeared he lived alone.

"May I ask what your dog's name is?

"That's my Brengi."

"Brengi's an unusual name; does it have any particular meaning?" The dog sidled up to Rowena, gently placing his face on her knee. Her heart warmed as she looked at the aged dog's face.

"I knew a mate once with the last name of Brengi. The definition means 'noble hound' in Cornish and indeed this old boy is. He's eleven though, and getting on in his years."

Mr. McGreevy stood up with the help of his cane. He motioned with his hand towards the kitchen. "I think supper is ready—ladies first."

He removed some magazines from a chair so Rowena could sit

down at his old country table. There were numerous newspapers stacked on the small hutch and counter. "I give my apologies for the massive clutter."

"It doesn't bother me in the least. I like your chaos; it indicates you are quite the bookworm."

"That I am. That I am indeed."

Rowena scanned her eyes around the cozy kitchen. An old tin tea kettle and iron skillet sat on top of the vintage stove. One wall had a wooden shelf lined with mason jars full of preserved food. Right below the supplies, blackened and dented pots and pans from years of use, hung from pegs. Around his sink draped a gingham curtain and a small galvanized bucket full of fruit sat on its sideboard.

Mr. McGreevy brought the hot stew over and put it in the center of the table. He pulled from the oven freshly baked corn bread. Brengi, snug under the table, leaned his back against her feet. She couldn't quite reach him with her hand. She slipped her shoe off and petted his back with her foot. When she absent mindedly stopped stroking him, he would nudge her leg with his nose.

With her stomach full from two bowls of stew and three slices of cornbread, Rowena got up to clear the table and take them to the sink. "That was absolutely delicious, thank you."

"You're quite welcome. Don't worry about cleaning up, I'll do it later."

"I better get back to the house; I've a lot to do in getting things in order."

"Of course, we'll be seeing each other." Mr. McGreevy stood at the stove and filled a container with leftovers, and then handed them to Rowena. "Here ya go, it's much more than I can eat."

"That's so kind of you, thank you again." As she walked to the door, Brengi followed her. She gently leaned down and scratched the scruff of Brengis's neck. "Goodbye 'ol boy." At the end of Mr. McGreevy's sidewalk she turned around and waved goodbye to her kind new neighbor.

Back home Rowena went to her bedroom and sat down at the desk, opening up her laptop computer. With her hotspot, she got online and checked her e-mails. She briefly got on Facebook and scrolled down the newsfeed, wondering if any of her friends were as alone as her at that moment.

Rowena went over to the window and pulled back the curtain and looked out onto the darkness. The moon shone onto the landscape and silhouetted the moors, a strange type of beauty she had never seen before.

Rowena walked back to her computer to turn it off and then pulled back the sheets on the bed. She crawled in and lay on her back with her forearm across her forehead.

Just as she drifted off to sleep, a noise above in the attic awakened her. She could hear a screech owl trilling and whistling outside the window. His noise helped sooth her.

As a little girl, her mother once told her a story from Greek Myology about owls. In the tale, the owl was a symbol of higher wisdom and the guardian of the Acropolis.

The memory of her mother reading those words brought her comfort, alone in her room that night.

The noise in the attic has to be my imagination.

And she drifted back to sleep, deeply, not waking up until morning.

Chapter Nine

Rowena walked across the lane and opened the gate door that lead to Mr. McGreevy's small chalet. A carport leaned up against the place with a vintage, chalky green Morris Minor parked inside. She continued up the flagstone walkway and knocked on his door. English Ivy was growing about the exterior stone walls of his home. A charming Rowan tree with bright red berries brushed up against the house. The small stoop leading to the front door had a galvanized bucket with garden tools. A Weeping Willow in the front yard looked graceful in the breeze as a baby red squirrel dashed up its trunk.

Brengi started barking from inside. Mr. McGreevy opened up the door and looked surprised. The dog's tail thumped against the door jamb as he came to greet her.

"Good morning, Mr. McGreevy. I hope I'm not intruding too early in the morning. I haven't had time to organize or clean anything in the house to cook. I'm going into the village to find some breakfast. Would you like to join me?"

"Well, young lady, considering I haven't had a date since my wife passed away, I would be a fool to turn down an offer like that." He reached inside the door for his woolen ivy cap and coat and grabbed his cane.

Rowena took Mr. McGreevy's arm and with her other hand bent down to pet the top of Brengi's head as he came outside to sit on the stoop. The brisk autumn breeze engulfed them as they walked to Rowena's blue rented Toyota Corolla. The leaves were crunching beneath their feet and she inhaled the fresh clean air. She helped maneuver the elderly man into the passenger side of the car.

"Over there, on the right is a nice café called the 'Alchemy and U', they have a good breakfast." Mr. McGreevy pointed with his crooked finger.

Rowena found a parking spot.

The café and restaurant was an eighteenth century building with a flat iron facade and a large bow window with barn sash glass. A sidewalk sign read, 'Karaoke—Wednesday nights—6 to 9'.

The windows on the second story of the establishment were

dressed with Priscilla curtains and flower pots hung with dianthus and ivy draping down from them.

Entering the restaurant through French doors, she understood how it got its name. All along the left side stood a long narrow wooden bar with bar stools. On the shelves behind the bar were many different beers, wines, liquors and non-alcoholic beverages. A chalkboard menu on the wall listed their espresso and specialty coffees.

Rowena and Mr. McGreevy found a table to sit at near the back by the buffet. A young female server came over to their table.

"Good morning. Hello, Mr. McGreevy so good to see you," greeted a tall, red-haired woman. She nodded hello to Rowena.

"Good morning to you, Patty. You are looking well, as always. I would like you to meet Rowena Mills. She is the niece to Dr. Hollister and my new neighbor. Rowena, I would like you to meet Patty."

Patty's blue eyes grew large, and she extended her hand. "It's so good to meet you. I heard you were here in Morcant. Welcome. My first introduction to Dr. Hollister came at my birth." She smiled and put two water glasses on the table. "She was a fantastic doctor and even sweeter as a person."

"Thank you so much for that. I actually never met her. And regret deeply I didn't."

"Patty is a writer. You two should hit it off." Mr. McGreevy added.

"Really? What kind of writing do you do?"

"It's just a hobby. Right now my fiancé Russell and I are working on a comic book." The restaurant started filling up with people. "We'll have to talk more about our writing later when it's not so busy. May I take your drink orders?"

Rowena smiled at Patty. "I'll take a dark, robust coffee and cranberry juice, please."

"I'll have my usual cup of hot tea, lovely."

Rowena gazed about the place at the unique tables, round shiny wooden tops with black iron bases. The chairs were black lacquered iron with cushioned seats, the floors a polished oak.

"Help yourself to the buffet table." Patty set their drinks down.

The buffet table included everything an English breakfast is noted for: scrambled eggs, English bacon, beans and different breads.

Rowena put modest amounts of food on her plate. Mr. McGreevy applied more on his plate than she would have imagined. After they sat down, she commented. "I notice this place doesn't offer artificial sweetener on the table."

"You don't use that stuff, do you? It's garbage as far as I'm concerned."

"No, I don't, just curious." Rowena smiled.

They enjoyed the rest of their breakfast in silence.

Patty came back to the table. "Would either of you like a refill?"

"Actually, if you two will excuse me for a minute, I think I'll go to the loo. Oh, yes, please refill my tea." Mr. McGreevy stood up with the help of his cane.

"Can I assist you to the door?" Patty asked the elderly man.

"Nope, I can make it, ladies."

"I'm fine, no refills for me." As Rowena spoke, a tall man with dark hair wearing running shorts breezed quickly past the front window. "Whoa," she said under her breath.

"I heard that." Patty laughed. "That's our local doctor, Harry Reader. He lives above his surgery, just down the street. Well, you would know of course, that's where your Aunt Maude practiced."

"Yeah, you don't say? From what I could see, he looks a smidgen like Cary Grant." Rowena's curiosity was aroused.

"He's quite nice, yes. I think he's about thirty-five years old and—not."

"Patty, excuse me, could I have a refill?" A man at the next table called over.

"Sorry, Rowena, I'll talk to you later." Patty went over to help the man.

Mr. McGreevy came back and sat down.

As he sipped on his tea, Rowena asked Mr. McGreevy about his late wife. "May I ask how long your wife has been gone?"

He set his tea cup down and remained silent for a moment. His brown spotted face turned solemn. "Twenty five years. She died of breast cancer. It wasn't detected early enough."

Mr. McGreevy's hands, bruised black and blue with protruding veins, rested on the table. Rowena reached over and lightly patted one of them.

"I met her right after the war. She came from a good family, near London. She was a librarian. Prior to meeting her, I have to admit I didn't read that much. But the only way I could catch her attention was to go into the library and check out books." A light came to his eyes. "Still, through the years she taught me the enjoyment of reading, and that you can travel anywhere you want to with books. I had never met a finer woman."

"Do you have any children?" Rowena asked.

"Annik, my wife, could never conceive. Our dogs were our children. We always had at least two dogs and usually a kitty somewhere hiding in the midst of things. Brengi is now my only dog and Crookie, of course, my cat."

"Brengi's such a nice dog." Rowena picked up her glass and drank the last of her cranberry juice.

"May I ask you, Rowena, a little about your life and what your plans might be?"

"As much as I'm ashamed to admit, I am recently divorced. After receiving the letter informing me about my father's Aunt Maude's death and her leaving Morwen Cottage to me, I sold everything that I own. I did it all in haste, which I've sometimes regretted.

"Do you have any children?"

Rowena became silent for a moment. "No, I don't have any children."

"Well, we all meet the fork in the road sometime in our lives. But I believe that no matter which path we take, our lives will be hallowed if we do it with the noblest of motives. So far, Rowena, you have taken every step yourself to get to where you are. I think you have and will make the right choices."

"What a kind thing to say."

"And just remember, after all, wherever you go, there you are."

Spending a day with Mr. McGreevy was indeed a day made. He was like being with and listening to a sweet grandpa—soulful, wise and patient and he helped lighten her heart.

Chapter Ten

After Rowena dropped Mr. McGreevy off at his house, she went home and up to her room. As she stood and looked out the window, she wondered about her dad's sister, Constance. Why didn't her aunt inherit this estate instead of her? Was her aunt or uncle still alive? After Rowena's dad passed away, her mother lost contact with Constance and her husband Sidney, who lived somewhere in Utah. They had an only son named Rodney, who she hadn't seen since early childhood. Rowena's mother had tried on occasion to get in touch with Constance but finally gave up after never getting any response.

Rowena wanted to find her cousin. She walked over to her computer and fished around on Facebook for a Rodney Luftra. She was almost certain she found him. His profile picture was an

Amine animation and no cover photo. Still, it stated his birthplace as Utah and current location as California. She clicked on his photos and friends and both sections were locked to the public, so she couldn't see anything. She sent a private message with the hope she'd found him.

> "Hello, Rodney,
>
> My name is Rowena Mills.
>
> I hope I'm not sounding presumptuous, but I think I'm your cousin. If so, I haven't seen you since we were little. I hope all is well with you. How are your mother and dad doing? My mother lost all contact with your family after my dad passed away. I would like to hear from you sometime.
>
> If I have the wrong person, my apologies and just delete this message.
>
> Most Sincerely,
> Rowena Mills."

She hit the send button, and paused before she sent a friend request.

Rowena went downstairs and outside to the back of the house. She started in on some yard work pulling weeds. Inside a small shed, she found a machete and started hacking away at the thick brambles around the back entrance. She stumbled on a tree root which caused her to trip. As she tried to catch her balance, the sharp blade came down on her right pinkie finger, partially severing the tip.

Stunned for a moment, she ran around the house into the front door and grabbed a clean rag and wrapped her hand, the tip, still hanging on by a piece of skin and tendon.

Rowena didn't even think to take her handbag, but grabbed her keys. She held her bound hand up against her chest as she rushed to the village.

Dr. Reader rushed into the patients' room where Rowena sat. He quickly took off her crude bandage and looked at the tip of her pinkie hanging.

"Ooh— ouch, young lady this looks quite painful." The doctor took her hand and put a basin under it. "This is going to sting a little." He poured a solution on the wound to clean it.

Rowena winced.

He studied her face for a moment. "I advise you to look the other way as I numb the area and then sew it back on."

She turned her face towards the wall and covered it with her good hand.

"I've wanted to meet you Rowena, but certainly not under these circumstances. Your Aunt Maude and I were great friends. She took me under her wing when I was fresh out of medical school." Rowena knew he was speaking to calm her.

Rowena listened to what he was saying, but her trembling kept her from answering back. She peeked with one eye through spread fingers at her hand for a second as he stitched, and became oddly embarrassed by her ragged, neglected fingernails. Her Beatles t-shirt now had a sizable blood stain on the front of it.

"I'm fairly certain your finger is saved. I'll prescribe something for the pain and a mild sedative to help calm you down." Harry went over to a cupboard and brought back a salve. "Here—put this antibiotic cream on twice a day." He looked into Rowena's eyes, as if to study them. "May I ask what you were doing?"

Rowena sat in her chair, her finger throbbing. She looked up at him. Even in pain, she noticed how striking and tall Dr. Reader was and how polished his manners. His soft brown eyes seemed reassuring. She took a deep breath to calm herself enough to speak intelligibly. "As you know, I have recently inherited my aunt's estate. It has become neglected, so whether I decide to sell it or live in it, I need to get it fixed up."

Dr. Reader hesitated for a moment, and then started writing the prescriptions out. As he wrote, she looked past his white rolled up sleeves to his tanned arms with dark hair. He wore a gold watch and she noticed he didn't have on a wedding ring.

When Rowena stood up, she became dizzy and took a hold of the desk for support.

"Are you alright?" He gently grasped her upper arm and for a second her nose brushed against his clean scented dark hair.

"Yes, I'll be fine." Rowena held up her bandaged hand. "Oh—and a million baby kisses for sewing me up."

Dr. Reader smiled as he handed the prescriptions to Rowena. "You're quite welcome."

"And I appreciate your kind words about my aunt."

As she started to walk out the door, he touched her shoulder. "I could suggest someone to help you. I know of a few good blokes."

Rowena turned around and looked up at him.

"With your permission, I'll send someone your way." He gazed into her face and moved his eyes down to the slight dimple on her chin, then proceeded to scan her body, stopping at the stain on her Beatles t-shirt.

Chapter Eleven

Sitting around the house for the past couple of days made Rowena anxious. Aunt Maude's television looked like something out of the sixties. The antenna that once set on top of the house now lay at a 90 degree angle on its perch pointing in the direction of hell. The only station it picked up was a fuzzy—Welsh soap opera called Pobol y Cwm. She went to her computer, checked e-mails, and then got on Facebook. Her cousin Rodney had accepted her friend request. He also sent a private message.

"Hello Rowena,

Yes, we are indeed cousins. I am greatly surprised to get a message from you. Yes, it's been a very long time since we've seen each other.

I'm sad to say I haven't been in contact with my parents for a while. Mom is a lonely, miserable woman who is her own worst enemy. Our relationship became toxic, and for my own sanity, I had to sever ties. I hate it that I can't see my dad, but to make peace, he goes along with mom.

By the way, how's your mother doing? Is she still living?

I need to go now but will keep in touch.

Take care,

Rodney"

Rowena sent a comment back, using her two index fingers to type.

"It is so good to hear from you. I'm sorry to hear about your relationship with your parents. Yes, we will keep in touch."

She included her email address and she hit the reply button. She then went to his profile on Facebook and clicked on the photos and found nothing, and then clicked friends, only two.

Hmm that's a bit strange.

She lay back on her bed. She couldn't bring herself to tell her cousin about her mother.

"Okay, enough of this sitting around and feeling sorry for myself."

She put a rubber glove over her injured hand and started the task of cleaning the house. Her finger throbbed as she got on her hands and knees to scrub the kitchen floor and wipe out the cupboards. She eyed the medication on the counter that she hadn't given in to. She made a resolve many years ago, after that hapless drug induced night, to never take drugs again, even if they might be necessary.

Somebody knocked at the door. It startled her out of her reverie and she didn't move for a moment. She went to the living room window and peeked out through a crack the curtain. She could make out a slim, dark curly haired guy of medium height wearing blue jeans and t-shirt.

"Yes, who is it, please?"

"Good morning, my name is Simon Eddy. Dr. Reader, who is a friend of mine, suggested I come here and ask if you need some help."

Rowena opened up the door and went onto the porch.

He had a genuine smile and seemed to be jovial.

"Yes, I could use some help, but my funds are limited. I can pay you 50 pounds a day."

"No worries ma'am, we can work that out later on. Dr. Reader has made arrangements with me. He is paying me for two full days of work."

"Are you serious?"

"Yes ma'am, doctor's orders." Simon smiled.

Simon tore into the yard with a vengeance. He had the back entrance way cleared off and the flagstone walkway looking pristine. It gave such encouragement to Rowena she tied back her long chestnut brown hair and started helping as best she could. She liked working with Simon.

"I see that you are married, Simon." Rowena looked at his gold wedding band on his hand.

"Yes, my wife Daisy and I have two children, a boy, Heath, who is eight and a girl, Heather, who is six." Simon took off his ball cap and wiped his forehead with a bandana.

"I worked for a contractor as a carpenter, but the company closed down. My wife, kids and I are temporarily living in a small section of my sister's home, a historical manor in the village."

"I'd like to meet your wife and kids." Rowena handed Simon a glass of iced tea.

After two full days of cleaning the yard in the crisp autumn air, the area looked transformed. And the workout invigorated Rowena. Color came back in her cheeks and her appetite returned to normal, even gaining a couple pounds. She started to recover her sense of equanimity.

"Thank you so much Simon. You'll never know how much this means to me. How would you like to continue helping me for a while? The interior really needs repairs. I insist on paying you here on out."

"I think we could work something out. I can talk to my wife. If you don't mind, she can help and is quite talented.

"I'd like that very much."

That evening as she finished up with supper a beating sound came from up above again. This time it wasn't her imagination. She found a flashlight and slowly ascended the stairs into the attic, listening to a racket going on. As she entered into the spacious loft, she spotted a closed off room down the hall. She crept to the door and listened, the noise coming from within.

Her heart pounding, she gradually opened the creaky door. With only the twilight shining through a window, she spotted something moving. She gasped, and held her hand to her heart as if to stop the pounding. And then she smiled.

A black crow fluttered around the room, cawing, more afraid than Rowena.

"Do you know you have scared the living day lights out of me?"

The window was open and unlatched. "Come on, poor little lost one; let's put you back with your family."

She opened the window wider and maneuvered him to fly out.

And then she latched the window shut.

Chapter Twelve

Rowena rose early the next morning, drove into the village, and arrived at Dr. Reader's office on time. As she sat in the waiting room, the smell of antiseptic filled her nostrils, making her slightly nauseous.

Should I mention to the doctor my bouts of queasiness and missed periods from months of nervous upset?

In the small examining room, the doctor leaned close. "Your wound is healing well. You'll have a scar, but just consider it your own unique tattoo." He lowered his long eye lashes as he finished dressing the wound. "Please know that if you ever need anything, feel free to call me." He smiled with gleaming white teeth and a dimple appeared on his cheek. "Anytime."

Did she detect something in his voice other than professional concern?

"Dr. Reader, I want to thank you for your generosity in regards to Simon helping me. I hope to repay you sometime. He did a wonderful job."

"You'd never need to repay me. I'm glad to help. And you are most welcome. Your Aunt Maude was like family to me, and I want to make sure you are doing alright."

Rowena got up to leave and started for the door. Dr. Reader patted her lightly on her shoulder and she caught the fresh scent of his cologne.

His warm gesture had softened her heart and sent a tremor up her spine.

"I appreciate your kindness. I'll definitely call you if I need something. But I think I'm fine for now. Mr. McGreevy, my neighbor and his dog, Brengi help keep me company and look after me."

Rowena walked out the door.

Keep your wits about yourself, Rowena. He's only your doctor. He's just a man, only a man. He is just a tall, handsome, intelligent, nice smelling, successful man.

Harry slipped off his sunglasses and stared out the window as Rowena sauntered down the street. Her long legs guided one foot in front of the other, and her hips swayed to the music in his mind.

She pulled back a lock of her long chestnut hair, the brilliant color captured in the sun.

I'd like to touch every strand.

Tables packed with fresh fruit and vegetables lined the walk at the market across the street. Rowena stopped in her tracks, and the hair on her arms stood up.

A man was purchasing some things at the market. He looked just like the hitchhiker who had helped her that pitiful night years ago. She waited for the traffic to pass and scurried across the street. But by the time Rowena got there, like a phantom in the shadows, the man had disappeared.

"It couldn't be him. In Cornwell? It has to be my imagination."

She shook it off and walked over to the Alchemy and U Café, looking back over her shoulder a couple of times. Inside, Rowena found a corner table.

As she sat down the server Patty brought her some water.

"Hi Rowena, it's good to see you."

"Hi, Patty. How's the writing going?" Rowena folded back the menu.

Patti turned her head from left to right, "I have a great scene written for Russell's super lizard."

Rowena laughed. "Sounds awesome. If you can spare a minute, I'd like to hear about it."

"Really? You want to hear about our comics? You're so sweet." Patty beamed. "Let me turn in your order first because I have something else I'd like to tell you."

Rowena handed Patty the menu. "Could I have a small coffee and egg sandwich, please?"

Patty brought Rowena her order. "It's time for my break; would it be ok if I sit down with you?"

"Of course you can. I'd enjoy your company."

Music played softly in the background. The breakfast crowd had left, and only one man remained at the bar.

"I have a good story to tell you about your aunt before she died. Several of us got together for her eightieth birthday and gave her a gift certificate for a day at the spa. Dr. Hollister wouldn't have indulged herself with such things. But word has it she completely enjoyed her mud facial." Patty covered her mouth and giggled.

"I sure wish I could have met my Aunt Maude. I appreciate hearing good things about her."

Rowena leaned over a bit and spoke softly. "I just saw a man at the outdoor market I swear is someone I know. Someone from my dark past, I am afraid to say." She described him in detail to Patty.

"No, that doesn't sound like anyone from the village." Patty leaned close to Rowena. "That man sitting over there at the bar is a real creeper. She whispered. "He's been seen off and on around town for a while."

Rowena discreetly peered over towards the bar.

"We get tourists around here a lot but they are usually open about where they are staying. I can't put my finger on it exactly, but something is off about him. I can't make out his accent. His clothes are frumpy and he smells badly." Patty shivered. "And he always keeps to himself."

"Do you have a boss or supervisor here at all times? You must be careful, Patty."

"Yes, Iggy, the owner is here most of the time. Oh, don't get me wrong, I'm not really scared or anything. Russell picks me up most of the time when I get off."

Rowena finished her meal and got up to leave. She spoke in a low voice. "See you later Patty. Please, take care."

Rowena went to the counter to pay her bill and glanced over at the man at the bar.

He was already staring at her. His piercing yet vacant eyes startled her. She quickly looked away.

Chapter Thirteen

Stepping out of the café, the afternoon sun warmed the autumn air and Rowena stood under an awning as she pulled out a water bottle from her handbag. A small car raced by and honked a long blaring beep at another pedestrian. Startled, Rowena rested her body against the building.

In a shadowed opening, four feet in front of her, two voices engaged in conversation, one standing, having an American accent, the other man sitting on a motorcycle. She put the lid back on the water and took quiet steps toward the dark space, waiting for their conversation to end.

Standing too close, she caught her breath as the American quickly turned around moving forward, and nearly bumped into her.

"Pardon me," he said.

"Wait." Rowena reached her hand out.

The style of his hair had changed. Shorter. His weight had increased a bit. But Rowena never forgot a face—not even a blurry one.

"I'm sorry to stop you. You wouldn't happen to be from the Mapletown Illinois area would you?"

He turned around and studied her with clear green eyes. That night long ago his eyes seemed murky, surreal. He took a step away from her and furrowed his brows. His gaze lingered before he answered.

"I went to college there for a short while. That's been close to twelve years ago. Were you a student there?"

Rowena didn't know how to begin. "Do you remember hitchhiking on the highway to Mapletown one moonless night? And a young girl picked you up? Only to get half way there when she became so sick you had to finish driving?"

The man didn't speak for a moment, his eyes darting around until they settled on a bicycle rack nearby. When his eyes returned to hers, he nodded without blinking. "Yes, I do remember that night. Embarrassed about that, are you?"

"Yes, I'm almost ashamed to admit it." Rowena's face blushed pink.

"I suspected you had taken some drugs. But my primary thought concluded something dreadful had just happened to you."

"A boyfriend problem is all. I cannot believe I have run into you. Do you know I went back searching for you, wanting to thank you? I couldn't find you and convinced myself you were a figment of my imagination. You are real, aren't you?" Rowena asked half kidding, half serious. "What in the world brings you to Cornwall?"

"I'm just traveling through Morcant for the day, on my way to St. Ivies. I have to be leaving shortly."

"Are you traveling alone?" Rowen tilted her head to peer into the space around the building. A couple walked by, holding hands.

He looked at the pair out of the corner of his eye. "Yes, I'm taking a break from my law practice back in Long Island New York and traveling through Europe." He pulled at the strings on his windbreaker. "May I ask what you are doing here in Morcant Cornwall?

"I've inherited a home here from a relative, a great-aunt."

He nodded. "I must be going now. By the way, that night after I drove you back and dropped you off by the cemetery, I couldn't find another person to pick me up. I had to walk all the way back to Mapletown."

"Oh no, I'm so sorry."

"No worries." He shook Rowena's hand. "Good bye, stay happy." He started walking away but turned around. "This is unbelievable running into you here like this. Don't you go picking up any more strangers, you hear me? That's a good way to get seriously harmed."

He smiled and started walking away. He got about a half a block down the street.

She ran after him. "Please stop for just another moment. I don't even know your name. My name is Rowena."

He stopped, turned around, looking Rowena in the eye. "I'm Hunter."

"Hunter you very likely saved my life." Tears leaked from her eyes and fell from her face. It may sound silly, but I know this is serendipity. I'll never forget you."

Before she had time to think, she put her arms around his neck and hugged him tightly. She clung to him as a sad child.

After a short time, he took his hands and gently unlatched her grip from around his neck. For a brief moment, he held her hands. He gave her a slight wink.

Hunter walked away, just as he had that dark night many years ago.

Chapter Fourteen

Repairs were in full swing. Simon had jacked up the sagging floor. Mr. McGreevy kept everyone fed with stew and Cornish pasties. Even Brengi stayed busy on Rowena's porch. He'd finished at least three pigs ears from a bag she'd purchased for him. And to her great surprise, one day as she drove up the lane, the television antenna stood straight up to the sky.

Rowena spent many hours scrubbing and polishing all the woodwork and floors. She did the same with the furniture. She'd washed windows and cleaned the curtains.

Simon's wife, Daisy, had helped at least three days a week. She knocked on the front door as she called Rowena's name.

"Around here," Rowena answered. At the side of the house, she bent over a shrub of English white roses, the last to bloom for the season, to gather for a table arrangement.

"Good job." Daisy smiled. "Add this one to the center." Daisy picked a stem from a red fern.

"You certainly have a knack for putting colors together." Rowena added the stalk to her flower bundle.

"As a child, my sisters and I would pick flowers and dry them to make bouquets. Then we sold them at the market." Daisy spoke softly with a lilt in her voice. Her long golden blonde hair flowed in the breeze, with lashes to match and freckles sprinkled on her face and arms.

"That sounds quite wonderful."

"It did have an effect on my decision for horticulture studies in college. And someday I'd like to open a shop."

"You are the girl who hears the music in the breeze and poetry in the wild flowers," Rowena said as they walked through the front door. "You're like Mother Earth herself."

Daisy's infectious optimism always filled up the room. "Wow—I'll take that as a compliment."

On occasion, Daisy, an exquisite cook and baker, prepared the meals. She or Simon would pick their kids up from school and bring them back to the house for supper.

Rowena's new friends were like family. One day she broke protocol and wanted to take them into the village for lunch.

"Everyone's been so wonderful in helping me out. Why don't

you let me treat all of you to a meal at the Alchemy and U? Iggy makes the best fried chicken I've ever tasted."

"That sounds good to me," said Simon.

"I second that motion," Daisy echoed.

"I'm sure Mr. McGreevy will be game to go."

Simon, Daisy, Rowena and Mr. McGreevy all loaded up in Simon's old SUV Honda and headed into Morcant for Iggy's magnificent fried chicken lunch special.

As they made the turn in town, on the left and down about a block, Simon noticed an area barricaded off with yellow caution tape. "I wonder what that's for."

Everyone turned their heads and looked in that direction.

"That area has a muddy old creek that streams through a gully," said Mr. McGreevy.

Entering, the café, the lights were low, tables empty. No smells came from the kitchen. The village police officer stood towards the back, talking to Iggy. *This isn't right.* Rowena's heart started pounding in her chest. An unspoken premonition whispered in her ear. She peered around the café for Patty. *Something has happened to Patty. Dear God no, please let me be mistaken.*

They took a seat at one of the large tables.

The owner, Iggy walked over to the table, his shoulders slumped, his blue eyes red-rimmed from crying. "I'm sorry, but we're closing for business today. I forgot to lock the front door. Patty's been missing for a couple of days." He choked, tried to compose himself, without much success. "We knew something was wrong because it wouldn't have been like her to just disappear." As if his legs could not hold him he knelt by the table. "This morning they found her body outside the village in a gully." Tears ran down Iggy's face. He pulled his half apron up to absorb the tears.

All at the table remained silent as Simon got up and offered a comforting arm to Iggy's shoulder. Rowena and Daisy shared a look of shock for a moment until she closed her eyes and stood. Questions in her mind screamed for answers."

"You mean she's in the hospital?" Rowena blinked away a vision of Patty's face pale and tortured. "I'll go see her."

Iggy shook his head. "No. Patty's…she's dead."

Rowena's chair fell back and scraped across the floor as she moved toward Patty's boss. "That can't be. Who would hurt her?"

Daisy took Rowena by the arm. "I'm sorry, honey. I'm so sorry."

"Her comic books. She has to finish them. No." Rowena burst into tears—her mouth went dry as water streamed from her nose and eyes.

"We should go," Simon suggested.

Mr. McGreevy pulled a napkin from the canister on the table and handed it to Rowena. He took another one to wipe his own tears.

They walked back to the SUV, in silence, the only sound being the doors shutting, the seat belts clicking. The drive back to the cottage seemed distorted, dreamlike. As Simon made the turn just outside Morcant, they peered again at the yellow tape surrounding the area by the gully.

"Who's that standing there?" Rowena asked as she cranked her head to look.

"Oh, no. It's Patty's fiancé, Russell." Daisy now burst into tears—she wiped her tears with her forearm.

Rowena covered her face with her hands. "I can't look. This is too horrible."

Simon finally spoke. "Rowena, you need to have someone stay with you. Mr. McGreevy, you shouldn't be alone either."

"Brengi will help look after me. I've a couple guns in the house I can dust off. Honey, I can get one ready for you to take home." Mr. McGreevy offered as his voice became tight from a lump in his throat.

"I don't have a clue how to use a gun. But if you show me, I'll keep it close by. No one needs to stay with me; I'll make sure the doors are all locked. Mr. McGreevy is close by."

With her voice shaking, Rowena added, "One day at the café, Patty pointed out a strange looking guy sitting at the bar. I could pick him out of a line-up anywhere."

Chapter Fifteen

The mid-day sun shone down on the moors as Simon brought Mr. McGreevy and Rowena back to Mr. McGreevy's house. Simon helped the elderly man out of the SUV and held onto his arm as they walked to the front door.

Mr. McGreevy stood at the front door as Simon came back to the SUV.

"Daisy and I are leaving for the day. We're going to the school to pick up the kids. Rowena, keep your phone close to you."

Daisy stepped out of the car. "I just can't believe it's true. Patty and I went to school together, such a sweet girl." She went over and hugged Rowena. "I don't feel right leaving you out here. You and Mr. McGreevy are more than welcome to stay at Simon's sister's house; there is plenty of room."

"We'll be alright.' Rowena held the car door open. "We have Brengi to help protect us and Mr. McGreevy will show me how to handle a gun."

"I'm too shocked to even compose my words to make any sense right now." Daisy got back into the SUV. She rested her elbow on the window edge and put two fingers on her forehead, closing her eyes.

Rowena closed the vehicle door and followed Mr. McGreevy into the house.

Mr. McGreevy disappeared for a moment and brought with him two dusty gun holders. He sat them on the kitchen table and pulled a 380 pistol from one of them.

"This is the cylinder where you load the bullets. And this is how you cock the trigger."

"My goodness, you sound so militant, Mr. McGreevy."

"Sorry, I forgot myself for a second. You're more than welcome to stay over here if you are afraid. I fought in the British Army during WWII. I shouldn't have expected you to know how to handle a gun right away. You don't have to take it if you are too apprehensive."

"No, no, I want to take it. I'll be alright. Just go through the steps a bit slower."

Mr. McGreevy showed Rowena again several times how to use the gun.

"Let me heat up a little corn beef and cabbage."

It dawned on Rowena she hadn't eaten since morning.

After their meal, Mr. McGreevy followed Rowena to the door and stood on his stoop, as she walked back to her home, gun to hand. She reached her front door and turned around to wave to him, then shut and locked her front door, closing out the world.

Rowena went to the living room window and looked outside. The clouds had drifted away and left in their place a cold, eerie sky surrounded by a small sliver of a moon. She closed the curtains tight, sealing any cracks.

Rowena reclined back in her chair, flipped on the lamp and started reading a book. The wind started picking up outside. The local weather man, for a change, had an accurate prediction and a storm moved in. She fell asleep with the book still in hand.

Rowena woke up to a sudden start. A hard object had hit the side of the house. The wind now whirled and whistled through the trees. An odd draft filled the house. She got up and crept around the different rooms.

Rowena passed by the door that entered into the attic and stopped. The draft blew from up there. She listened, and then spotted a flashlight on one of the stairs; she ascended into the loft.

Entering into the spacious area, the repetitive sound of a loose shutter kept hitting the side of the house. The door down the hall that led into the small enclosed room was ajar and it kept opening and closing with each thrust of wind. She grabbed ahold of the knob with trepidation and went inside. The old dusty curtains were blowing straight out, horizontally. The window stood wide open.

Her heart thumped so hard it made a roar in her ears as she promptly closed and latched the window. She swiftly walked down the stairs and into the dark kitchen.

What do I do now? I left the gun in the living room. She could hear Brengi barking in the distance. *Do I hear another noise? Is it just the wind?*

She listened again. A knocking noise came from the front door. She stood paralyzed, her heart now throbbing in her head. And then a loud voice, "Rowena!" The knocking came again, now faster and more urgent.

"Rowena, it's me Harry Reader."

With stealth, she took small steps while making her way back to the living room, grabbed the gun and peaked through a crack in the curtain. A shadow cast a figure under the porch light.

"Prove it's you." Rowena called through the closed door.

"When I first met you I sewed up your pinkie finger. You had on a bloody Beatles t-shirt, not that the Beatles are bloody; I mean your top had a red stain on it. Your hair was in a haphazard ponytail and your shoes were brown crocs. And if I might add you needed a manicure. The second time I saw you, you wore a peasant style dress. "

Rowena's eyes opened up wide, and she smiled with a sigh of relief. *"Wow, vivid memory."*

Rowena slowly opened up the door, her heart still thrusting with adrenaline, but immensely happy to see Dr. Reader. "Please come in."

He looked at the gun in her hand and nervously ran his fingers through his thick dark hair. "Um— would you mind terribly putting that thing down?"

"Oh, sorry, Mr. McGreevy loaned it to me." Rowena laid the gun on the table.

"I'm sorry to come out here so late. And I especially regret to have frightened you so. Everyone is on edge because of what happened to Patty. I just heard talk at the pub a vagrant was seen not too far from here, carrying a sack over his shoulder. When the police followed up on the sighting, they couldn't find anyone. I wanted to make sure you were alright. And I'm relieved you are."

"Actually, I'm a bit freaked out right now. A while back I let a crow out that was flying around in my attic. He came in through an open window up there. I remember distinctly latching it shut after letting him out. Long story short, I went up into the attic just now, and the same window was open again."

"Are you sure? Do you think it's possible through all of the renovations you've been doing that Simon or Daisy could have been up there and forgot to latch the window?"

"That's a reassuring thought. That must be what has happened. But just to be sure, will you go through the house with me to check every room?" Rowena looked up at Dr. Reader, her eyes pleading.

"Of course." Harry briskly ran his hand up and down Rowena's arm in a calming gesture.

Together they inspected every space in the house, and then walked up into the attic; Rowena following close after Dr. Reader. The warmth of his aura surrounded her, and from behind, she couldn't help noticing how nicely his jeans fit his body—*and why are his athletic shoes so endearing? I mean, after all, half of the male population wears the same kind.*

Harry opened the door to the enclosed room and went to the window and observed around it. "Come here, look at this. There's a dirty finger print on the sill."

Rowena walked over to inspect it. "It must be from Simon or Daisy. I'll ask them about it Monday."

"Everything else seems to be in order." Dr. Reader said after he scoured the house a second time." All your windows are locked, including the cellar door. I'm giving you my private phone number." He took a note pad and pen from his pocket and wrote it down.

Rowena borrowed his pen and jotted down her number in exchange.

He sauntered to the front door, and then turned around, lingering for a moment, taking in Rowena with his eyes and then gliding his gaze to her hair, as if studying each shiny strand. "Please give me a call anytime day or night if you feel afraid. And please, call me Harry."

"Thank you, Harry, I will."

She shut the door. *Why does he have to be so damn good-looking? And his charming self doesn't have a clue he is.*

She lay back again in the recliner and bundled up to her neck with a warm blanket.

It suddenly occurred to her that she only had on a nightgown.

Chapter Sixteen

The next morning Rowena made herself oatmeal for breakfast. Simon and Daisy wouldn't be coming today on Sunday. She took her coffee upstairs and sat at the computer, checking her email. The inbox had a new message from Rodney.

> *"Hi Cousin,*
> *What's up? Not much going on here.*
> *I hope someday to see you again. We could have a cousin reunion.*
> *Are you married or with anyone?*
> *You didn't mention your mother; I hope things are ok with her.*

I will close for now, but you take care in that magical land of Cornwall.

Your cousin, Rodney."

Rowena sat there, her mind wrestling with itself. She glanced through her other emails from Rodney. Just as she had thought, she never mentioned she was in Cornwall. Her profile on Facebook stated she lived in Sandburg, Illinois. *"How could he have known?"*

She hit reply. And then backed out.

Rowena got dressed and walked over in the crisp morning air to visit Mr. McGreevy.

"Would you like a cup of hot tea?" Mr. McGreevy reached into his cupboard for a tea cup.

"That sounds wonderful. The mornings are getting quite chilly." Rowena rubbed her cold hands together as she sat down at the kitchen table.

"I've just made some baked Scotch Eggs." He scooped one up with a spatula and put the food on a plate. He placed it in front of Rowena.

"*That* looks delicious. I hope you know your kitchen is becoming one of my favorite spots on earth."

"I'll accept that accolade and run with it." He smiled and sat down. "So, what's on your mind this morning?"

"Dr. Reader paid me a visit last night. He is concerned about me staying out here alone."

Mr. McGreevy passed her a napkin. "That's very attentive of him. I hope they find who did this beastly crime. Patty was a lovely girl."

"I'm still in shock. It's just terrible. Yes, she was lovely." Rowena picked at her napkin and started twisting the cloth between her fingers.

They finished eating in silence.

Rowena took her plate to the sink and sat back down. "The strangest thing happened to me this morning."

"What strange thing is that?" Mr. McGreevy asked.

"I've reconnected with a cousin, via email and Facebook. He's the son of my dad's sister. I've only told a couple of close friends, my aunt, and uncle, that I'm in Cornwall. But my cousin knows I'm here."

"Maybe he contacted one of your friends on Facebook."

"I suppose that is possible. And my ex-husband knows I'm here. He may have somehow connected with him. Wow, I'm impressed with your astuteness about social media."

"I watch the news."

"At any rate, you are probably right. I'm just being a little paranoid."

"Not to change the subject, but you have never mentioned your mother."

Rowena sat silent for a moment, and then cleared her throat. Tears welled up in her eyes.

Brengi came over and laid his head on her lap.

"There now, child. Take all the time you need."

"My mother had breast cancer and test results actually showed the disease hadn't spread. But after they performed the breast surgery, she never woke up from the anesthesia."

"How dreadful. Could they explain to you why that happened?"

"Going back to the day my dad was killed, my mother unfortunately didn't escape injuries either. She sustained a severe head trauma. The doctor explained that due to the skull injury she possibly developed early onset dementia. And sometimes major surgery will cause the disease to accelerate into the final stages."

Brengi looked up at Rowena. She patted his head.

"I had to put her in a nursing home. She passed away two months before my divorce became final."

"Words cannot express, my dear, how sorry I am right now." His voice conveyed condolence. "But I do know that when my beloved Annik passed away, I thought I'd never go on with life. Someone once told me with very good intentions that I should just take one day at a time. Well, I went many months taking only two hours at a time, then four hours. Gradually I got to the one day at a time."

"Yes sir, sometimes life can dole out some pretty wicked stuff. And to be honest, I got to the 'one day at a time' only after I came here to Cornwall."

Chapter Seventeen

"The strangest thing happened Saturday night. I noticed an open window up in the attic. You wouldn't know anything about that would you?" Rowena asked as she walked toward her car.

Simon and Daisy looked at each other.

"No, I haven't been up in that room." Simon took off his hat and scratched his head.

"I haven't either. That sounds a bit scary."

"Dr. Reader came by to check to see if I was alright. We walked around the house together looking in all of the nooks and crannies. On the sill of the window, I just mentioned, we found a dirty finger print. I suppose the smudged marks could have been there already. But I remember latching that same window the first night I stayed here." Rowena leaned her back up against the car.

"I still think you should come and stay with us," Daisy said.

"Someone spotted a vagrant close to this area. I've seen the police scouting this region. I'm sure I'll be fine." Rowena climbed into her car. "I'm running into the village for some things. I should be back later today."

Rowena drove to the pharmacy to purchase vitamins and walked down to the open market for fruits and vegetables. As she put them in the trunk of her car, she noticed Dr. Reader going into the Alchemy and U.

The aroma of grilled food filled the air. She'd missed lunch and sauntered into the café, casually.

Harry motioned for her to join him at his table. He stood up as she came toward him, then pulled out a chair for her to sit in. "How are you today, Rowena?" He smiled and helped her scoot her chair back in.

"Thank you, Harry. I'm doing well but still a bit creeped out about the other night. I don't think I thanked you properly for coming all the way out to my house and checking on me." Rowena put her hand bag and laptop case on the empty seat next to her.

"The pleasure is mine. If only the visit could have been under a better setting."

"Actually, I'm not used to living in such a remote area. The property is lovely, but a little out of touch." Rowena glanced nervously around the café. "This place seems sad and empty in here without Patty."

"I know what you mean. I come in here most days for lunch. Patty could always put a smile on your face." Harry sighed and placed his hands behind his head.

The sound of a soulful blues piano virtuoso played softly in the background.

"I'll say one thing about Iggy; he has good taste in music. Speaking of him, I hope he's doing better—"

A waitress came over to the table with water and handed them menus. Her name tag read 'Kara.' "I'll be back to take your orders." She gave Harry a flirty glance and then a bit of a scowl to Rowena.

Harry looked up at Kara. "Thank you." After Kara walked away, he focused again on Rowena. "Kara has taken over for Patty. A bit scattered brained I'm afraid."

Rowena glanced through the menu and closed the cover. "It's probably rough on her knowing she is compared to Patty."

Harry changed the subject. "Your Aunt Maude told me after she moved from London to Cornwall to set up her medical practice, her younger brother, your grandpa, would come to spend summers with her."

"Yes. I remember my Grandpa Mills telling stories about his life in England."

"I suspect your Aunt Maude helped your grandpa with his dream to come to the United States. He was ten years younger than her and when their parents passed away, she became a surrogate mum," Harry recalled.

"My Grandma Deborah and Grandpa Jack moved back to England when I was seven years old. I remember one time before they left, grandpa constructed a 'kiddie condo' for me out of cardboard. I had more fun with those boxes than any fancy toy."

"Maude always spoke of your grandpa in the most endearing terms."

Kara appeared at the table and asked. "Have you decided what you want?"

"I'll have today's special of fish and chips, Kara," Harry said.

"The house salad, please, with honey mustard dressing." Rowena handed back the menu.

"My Grandma Deborah passed away when I was fifteen, and we couldn't fly over for the funeral, too expensive. Two years later grandpa sent word he wanted to attend my high school graduation. But one month before my graduation, we received urgent news he died suddenly of a heart attack. I did, however, find comfort in the idea that he *wanted* to be there for me." Rowena stared at a spoon on the table.

"That must have been quite sad. Maude said your grandpa was a good bloke."

"How kind of you to say, thank you."

Kara brought their plates of food. She bent forward to reveal large ample breasts, one with a butterfly tattoo, pushing out the top of her too tight blouse.

After Kara walked away, Rowena gave Harry a side glance.

"What?" Harry feigned innocence.

"Okay, on to the next subject. When I chatted with Mr. Chapman he told me you are from Birmingham and educated in Scotland. What brings you here to Morcant Cornwall?"

"While I was still in college, I became engaged. After graduation, we had a home purchased, and the wedding was in the definite planning stages. And then she was killed in a car accident. I guess I needed to get away from everything. I started looking for a place to start up a practice and Morcant was looking for a new doctor."

"I'm so sorry. I truly hope the best for you."

Dr. Reader nodded while wiping his napkins across his lips. "A horrible time for me."

"Morcant is very fortunate to have someone like you." Rowena studies the doctor's face as he looked down at his plate.

"Thank you." Dr. Reader looked up into Rowena's eyes.

They both were silent for the rest of their meal.

As they were finishing up, cool air rushed in as the door opened. A tall, handsome man with yellow hair entered the restaurant. He went to sit at the bar.

Harry leaned in and whispered. "That's the guy who was engaged to Patty. The authorities have put him through the wringer. He seems—" Kara came to the table and refilled their water glasses.

Harry glanced at his watch. "Oh, I need to get back to the surgery. I will talk to you later." He stood up, excused himself and went to pay his bill.

"Could I have my bill, please?" Rowena asked when Kara came to get the empty plates.

"Dr. Reader paid for your lunch," Kara said in a somewhat miffed voice.

Kara went over to Russell as he sat at the bar. He quickly downed a mug of dark ale, and then put the empty glass on the counter. It didn't escape Rowena's notice that Kara momentarily caressed the back of his neck.

Rowena opened up her computer. She decided to email Rodney back. She tied in with the restaurants Wi-Fi.

> *"Hello again, Rodney,*
>
> *You had asked about my mother. Sadly, she passed away earlier in the year.*
>
> *I'm very curious about something. How did you know I'm in Cornwall?"*
>
> *More later, Rowena.*

Just as she sent the email off, she heard a ding informing her she had a new email in her inbox. William. She quickly sat up straight in the chair and read:

Dear Rowena,

I never realized when you moved away how much I would miss you. How much I love you. I just can't stop thinking about you. We can have a fresh start together again. I am sorry for everything, my darling. You once said: a writer doesn't get it right with their first draft; she must rewrite a final one. Won't you please, Rowena, rewrite your final draft, with us together, forever?

Most sincerely,
William

Rowena's fingers shook as she started a mindless reply but her mind was muddled. At that moment she had no words.

Rowena put her handbag and computer case on her shoulder and started to exit the front door, stopping for a brief moment to look at her reflection in the glass. Her clothing didn't fit well; the loose material hung around her middle in a shapeless form. She buttoned up her black double-breasted trench coat and cinched the belt.

Someday, maybe, I'll buy something stylish.

Chapter Eighteen

Rowena shook off her glumness and looked down the street at Peter Chapman's building. She walked over to his office.

She could hear him on the phone as she entered. He looked up and cut his conversation short, then hung up. He stood to greet her.

"Good afternoon Mr. Chapman. Sorry to just walk in like this but I have a quick, curious question to ask you."

"Please have a seat." He gestured to the chair next to his desk and then sat down himself. "What can I help you with?"

"My deceased father has a living sister. Do you know anything about her? I'm surprised she didn't inherit Maude Hollister's estate."

Mr. Chapman sat there quietly.

More questions poured out of Rowena. "Why would the

inheritance go to me alone? Not to mention dad's sister has a son named Rodney. Wouldn't he have some entitlement?"

Mr. Chapman's eyes shifted back and forth. "Yes, to be perfectly honest with you I know about your Aunt Constance. I didn't mention anything to you on our last visit because I didn't think it was necessary."

"Not necessary? Why?" Rowena became distracted for a moment when Peter repetitively tapped his shoe against his desk.

"Four years before Maude passed away, Constance and her husband Sidney came over to England to pay her a visit. They tried manipulating her into leaving her estate and bank account to them."

"What an awful thing to do."

"Maude had a heart of gold and would give the shirt off of her back to anyone in need. But Maude was nobody's fool. She saw right through them."

Rowena shifted in her chair, incredulous.

"Then both of them came to me, trying to convince me that Maude was getting senile. They had the nerve to ask for guardianship over her."

"I'm guessing Maude would have no part of that."

"You have that right. After they left England, Maude came into my office to revise her will. Greediness can sure back fire. Prior to her revisal, Constance and your mother were the two living relatives on the will.

"I call that karma."

"After Maude passed away, procedures were set in motion to contact your mother. Through the confusion of wrong addresses and incorrect phone numbers, the process took three years to find your mother. By the time we found her, she had already passed away in a nursing home. The nursing home gave me your address. Well, you know the rest."

"Thank you for telling me this. I know their son Rodney hasn't had anything to do with them in a long time. Maybe it's no mystery why. Somehow though, my cousin knows I'm in Cornwall."

Mr. Chapman considered. "I hope he doesn't give you any trouble over the estate."

"I hope not either. By the way, I have two wonderful people helping me fix up Maude's house. The place is really transforming. Thank you so much for confiding with me."

The afternoon sun helped warm the chilly day. Rowena buttoned up her coat. All at once the sound of a throaty car jostled the stillness, and she turned to look.

Harry came down the street driving a dove gray Jaguar with silver wired wheels. The charcoal colored seatbacks sat high behind the dash.

Did I also notice a woman riding shotgun in the car? He went by so quickly she wouldn't be sure.

She stood still, watching, for a lingering moment, and then

walked to her car. As she went to open the door, she stopped in her tracks.

Walking down the street, Hunter appeared again. She yelled over to him, "Hi, Hunter."

He stopped, turned around at the sound of Rowena's voice and walked over to her. His blue jeans stuck out from the bottom of his black double breasted woolen overcoat.

"I'm surprised to see you again." Rowena's hair blew in the wind and she rearranged it with her hands, pulling the wavy long strands over to one side.

"I'm passing back through on my way to London." He looked down at the ground for a moment and wobbled both feet up and down as if keeping beat to some unheard music.

"Honestly Hunter, I would like to know a little more about you. You are somewhat of an enigma, you know. What do you specialize in with your practice?"

"I work mostly with boring things like wills and lawsuits, sometimes divorces." He motioned for Rowena to sit on a nearby bench. "Tell me a little about you. What ever happened to that poor little girl I met that night on the road? It appears things are going well for you now."

"To tell you the truth, I want to forget that night. You witnessed me at my very worst. Sometimes I think if a person is lucky enough to survive such stupidity, there is a great lesson to be learned."

"You mentioned last time you were having boyfriend troubles.

But let me guess, you went ahead and married the jerk who broke your heart. Yes? And now, of course you are divorced from him."

"How would you have known that I married and divorced him?" Rowena's voice went a higher pitch.

"I didn't know that of course. I've just seen this sort of thing quite often in my practice. Someone is beaten down emotionally and then they go back to the abuser. Don't be defensive. A lot of us have been there."

"I'm sorry. You just startled me for a second."

"We seem to meet each other coming and going, and once again, I have to leave now. I'm truly glad to know things are good for you."

Rowena was both intrigued and troubled by this man named Hunter.

Could he be a figment of my imagination or possibly an angel unaware?

The sunny skies gave way to a cloud cover and a mist started to fall. Rowena looked up at the sky and her face and hair became wet.

I don't mind the mist. No, I don't mind it at all— I like the rain.

Chapter Nineteen

Early the next morning Simon came alone to Morwen Cottage. He brought a truckload of firewood. As he threw the logs on the woodpile, he noticed the hatch on the exterior cellar door was ajar.

He went around and knocked on the front door.

Rowena grabbed a housecoat to put on and opened the front door.

"Rowena, sorry to bother you so early, but as I was piling up the wood, I noticed your cellar door is slightly open. The padlock on the hatch is unlocked. Did you happen to go down there?"

"I've never been in the cellar. I once opened the door from the kitchen and looked down from the top of the stairs, but didn't enter."

"I went into the basement when I jacked up the floors but I

made sure I put the key to the padlock back on the peg in the kitchen after I finished."

"You did that quite a while ago. I'm sure one of us would have noticed it unlocked."

They walked around to the cellar door, and Simon opened it up.

Rowena whispered. "I'm not letting you go down there alone. Come back inside with me while I get Mr. McGreevy's pistol. We can go into the cellar from the kitchen."

"Look, the padlock key is missing from the peg." Simon pointed to the pegboard by the interior cellar door.

As they slowly descended the rickety wooden stairs, cobwebs enveloped Rowena's face, sticking to her hair. Only a dim lightbulb at the foot of the stairs lit the dark. Simon pulled a flashlight out of his back pocket.

The dirt floors smelled very dank. Simon scanned the place. "Look over here, a hidden door."

Simon threw his light on a rounded, wooden door with decorative hardware, now rusty and loose. "The barrel bolt is unlatched." Simon looked at Rowena, both their faces ghoulish in the strange light.

"Do you suppose we could be walking into some kind of odd fairy tale?" Rowena asked as her fear was now mixed with intrigue.

"Wow—I couldn't say. Maybe some Trolls live in there." Simon chuckled a little to try and make light of the situation.

The door creaked as Simon slowly opened it. He pointed the

flashlight inside; a tunnel came into view, about twenty-feet long. At the other end they could see another door.

Simon entered first, Rowena following. They crouched, walking the five foot tall tunnel. The second door did not have a lock. The wooden structure opened into a six by eight foot vaulted room, with the ceiling about six feet at the peak.

"This must be where potatoes and other produce were stored long ago, a secret summer kitchen; or possibly a hiding place or bunker of some sort. My guess is your aunt had this built as a bomb shelter during WW II." Simon cast his eyes on the inside of the chamber.

"What a harrowing time for the people of Great Britain and the allies back then." Rowena shivered and looked around at the dusty cobwebbed walls and floor. "Do you think my aunt—wait... look over there!" She gasped and pointed at one corner in the room. There laid a dirty canvas back pack.

They peered into the bag to see a pair of jeans, a grubby t-shirt and a small notebook computer.

Simon got his tool box from his vehicle. He went back to the cellar and locked the interior barrel bolt on the door leading outside, then nailed four inch nails all around the perimeter. Together they scoured every corner of the house and nailed shut any window that didn't have a lock on it.

Simon and Rowena drove into the village to the police station.

Rowena handed the backpack to the officer by the name of Henry. "I'm completely terrified right now. Also, someone opened up my attic window a while back and left a dirty finger print."

"We'll come out directly to take the finger prints." Officer Henry assured Rowena.

"Thank you, Officer."

Officer Henry hesitated before he spoke. "Um, ma'am, I'm so sorry to bring more startling news, but um, there has been another murder."

"What?" Rowena rubbed her arms.

"Oh, dear God no—someone from the village again?" Simon grabbed his phone out of his pocket to call Daisy.

"I'm afraid so, chap. A young woman by the name of Kara Mullenson bludgeoned in her bed last night."

"You mean Kara from the Café?" Rowena became light headed and placed both hands to her skull, feeling the heat radiating from her scalp.

"Yes, indeed, it is. And young lady, you've no business staying out there alone in your house. At least until we can to the bottom of these murders."

"Yes, sir, I'll stay with my neighbor, Manchester McGreevy. I'll be safe with him."

"Just to warn you, we plan to have a couple of undercover detectives staking out your area."

"Do you have *any* leads on this?" Simon asked his friend.

Officer Henry said in a low voice. "Just between you and me, I think we got some pretty good DNA evidence at the scene. Kara's bedroom window had been opened and we found a shoe print on the floor. They're the same prints that we found around the crime scene of Patty. Plus a trace of skin cells under both of their fingernails."

Simon and Rowena drove back to the house. "I better get home. I'm worried about my family."

Simon walked with Rowena over to Mr. McGreevy's house to make arrangements for her to stay there.

"Take Brengi with you while you gather your things." Mr. McGreevy said.

Brengi and Simon walked Rowena to her front door. "I'll wait here with Brengi while you get what you need."

"Thank you Simon. I appreciate that."

As Simon walked with Rowena back to Mr. McGreevy's he said, "It'd be a good idea to teach the old guy how to use a cell phone."

"Yes, I do think that's a good idea. And Simon, let's don't worry about the house for a while. We can hold off on further renovations until things get sorted out."

Before Rowena went inside Mr. McGreevy's house, she placed her knapsack down and sat on his stoop, opened up her laptop and connected the hotspot, to e-mail her Aunt Agnes.

> "Hi Aunt Agnes,
>
> Sorry I haven't communicated more. I know they say a poor excuse is better than no excuse, but I have been busy over here in Cornwall getting this house ready.
>
> The time is drawing near where a decision has to be made on what to do. Even though I am only two months into my six month visa, things need to be put in order.
>
> I can't wait for you to come over here. You will fall in love with this place.
>
> I miss you and Uncle Robert terribly. I miss grandpa too. It is so kind of you to take him in to your home, instead of a nursing home.
>
> I am planning on coming back to the states after the first of the year.
>
> Please give Robert and grandpa a hug for me.
>
> > I love you xxx,
> > Your niece, Rowena."

Rowena hoped her aunt hadn't got wind of the murders. If she did, she would be on the next flight to England.

"Oh please Aunt Agnes, don't watch the BBC news."

Rowena glanced over at her house, the front porch light left on. She stood up with all her gear. "Come on Brengi, let's go inside."

Chapter Twenty

"You are more than welcome to sleep in my bed. I can sleep on the sofa." Mr. McGreevy offered.

"No, thanks, that is considerate of you but I'll be fine on the sofa."

"It's a bit reassuring knowing two detectives are outside at the moment."

"Yep, Officer Henry instructed me to leave my car unlocked so one of the undercover men could hide inside. The other man is hiding in my back yard; plus an unmarked car is down the lane hiding behind some bushes." Rowena hugged her chilly arms.

Mr. McGreevy brought out a woolen afghan that Annik had crocheted and laid it on the sofa. Rowena curled up and covered her body, the warmth engulfing her, even as the blanket smelled musty and was covered in cat hairs.

"Here's a hot cup of tea. The moors can get rather chilly at night." He handed the drink to Rowena, and then sat down on his chair, holding his own tea.

Crookie, his orange tiger cat, peeked slyly around the corner; normally a recluse, his curiosity had gotten the better of him. He never had to share his sofa with anyone.

"You know, I can't help but wonder about my dad's sister, Aunt Constance. I find the whole sorted mess hard to believe. How could she be so underhanded in regards to Maude's estate?" Rowena rearranged her blanket as she explained her conversation with Peter Chapman.

"Unfortunately, dealing with the greedy is part of life."

"But I'd like to think even the self-centered have a good side." Rowena put a strand of hair behind her ear.

"I'd like to think that too. But it seems to be embedded deep within some."

"I remember once listening to a zany radio call-in program. They posed a question to the listening audience. 'What is the most outrageous thing you have ever heard a preacher say?' One woman called, explaining a funeral she attended of a person of questionable character. The preacher doing the funeral service didn't know the deceased personally, but he walked over to the casket, looked at the family, and then shouted 'This man is going straight to hell!'

"The preacher didn't think that one through." Mr. McGreevy stifled a grin.

"No, he sure didn't, and a completely unforgivable thing to say. I thought back to a funeral I had once attended of someone whose scruples were sometimes in question."

"You had a similar experience?"

"No, perhaps a comparable person, but the preacher handled the situation quite differently. A nice obituary had been written. It became apparent through the preacher's words someone had taken the time to find some redeeming qualities in this person's otherwise capricious life." Rowena paused for a moment to sip her tea.

"Please, finish the story, I find this interesting." Mr. McGreevy sat his empty cup on the end table.

"I looked over and noticed a friend of mine sobbing. I surprised myself, digging in my own handbag for a tissue. I realized at that moment my friend had written the eulogy."

"Your friend did a noble thing."

"You know, I think it's important to humble ourselves to see things that are not particularly of our own view. Let those without sin cast the first stone."

"That's a very intuitive thing for you to say." The elderly man put his hand over his mouth as he yawned. "And I hope someday, you may have dialogue with your aunt."

Mr. McGreevy got up and started turning the lights off. "Good night, for now, I haven't stayed up this late in years." With his cane in hand, he shuffled off to bed.

Rowena laid there in the dark, quietly, with a smelly lumpy sofa pillow under her head. Her mind drifted to her ex-mother-in-law, Abigale. *What could have made her so damaged? Had something tragic or unspeakable happened to her as a child to irreversibly scar her?* The thought profoundly saddened her.

Crookie suddenly jumped up on the sofa to stake his claim. Visibly annoyed, he settled on the arm rest of the sofa, at Rowena's head, his loud purr roared in her ears. As she started to doze, he nipped at her hair, miffed as she slept in his favorite spot.

Brengi lay at the front door, sleeping, ready to slay the dragons if necessary.

Chapter Twenty-one

The next morning, the smell of bacon frying woke Rowena and her stomach growled.

Mr. McGreevy offered her a seat at the breakfast table and held a cup of coffee under her nose. Rowena inhaled the fresh aroma.

Rowena took the last bite of her toast and pushed the empty plate aside just as her mobile phone rang. She reached over to the hutch and picked it up.

"Hi Daisy, what's up."

"Good morning. I'm afraid I have some disturbing news. It's in today's newspaper."

Rowena sat up straight in her chair. "What disturbing news?"

"It appears Kara had two different boyfriends, one of them is allegedly Dr. Harry Reader."

Rowena's stomach started to churn. "I don't know if I believe that assumed story.

The day I had lunch with him in the Alchemy and U, he appeared rather annoyed with her."

"I don't know whether to believe it either. I asked Simon if he knew if Harry and Kara had a thing going and he just shrugged his shoulders. The police are questioning another guy, Russell, Patty's fiancé."

Rowena mind raced in different directions. *She remembered watching Kara rubbing Russell's shoulder that one day in the restaurant.* "Daisy, this is all ghastly."

"I know what you mean. Please, you and Mr. McGreevy take care; the nights can be quite desolate in the moors. Gotta go for now. I'll talk to you later. Bye."

"Bye. I'll talk to ya later."

"That conversation didn't sound like good news." Mr. McGreevy walked into the room.

"I hope there's nothing to worry about, Mr. McGreevy. More suspects. Will this ever end?"

Rowena went to the living room and sat on the sofa, to open up her laptop and check her e-mail. Inbox: Agnes Trueheart.

Hello Rowena,

Well, slap me silly, my niece has returned from the abyss. We thought maybe you fell into the fifth dimension or something.

It's so good to hear from you. Robert and I have been reading up on your location, and we are fascinated. If we ever get over there, we have a list of things we want to see. Have you ever heard of the South West Coast Path National Trail? Robert and I have taken up walking, and that area is now on our bucket list.

We saw William this morning; he appeared harried, pulling a suitcase. Still, he asked about you. His girlfriend must have dumped him—no comment lol.

Grandpa is doing well but got fairly furious when he noticed my new tattoo. I bent over, and my shirt slipped up a bit. If he hadn't been struck in his wheelchair, I think he would have dropped kicked the Sunday ham into the fireplace.

So sweet though, I went in the other night to his room, and he had fallen asleep reading. He uses the birthday card you sent him as a bookmark.

You take care. We're sure you are plenty busy. You are in my thoughts often.

Bye, for now, honey, oxox

Rowena minimized the letter. *Thank heavens Agnes hasn't got word about the murders over here.*

She went back to the email William had sent her. With sweaty palms she guided the mouse and hit reply.

Hello, William,

I must say I was speechless when I opened your e-mail, also a little flattered at first. But that is what our relationship has always been with you. Do you realize I have only heard those words from you after you have tired of your foolishness?

But I don't totally blame you. We should have parted years ago. I foolishly hung on after the candle of our romance had burned out. I only pretended, because you see, I don't love you and I haven't in a long time.

Obviously, things aren't going well with the new woman in your life; give love a chance, I know in time, you will find your perfect goddess somewhere.

You have asked me to rewrite the words again. I have rewritten my final draft, but sadly, you are not in them. I am not sure yet what I plan to do. But I am coming back to the States after the New Year.

We definitely need to talk...

Rowena got up and symbolically shook herself as if to shake off the dust of her past. "Mr. McGreevy, I am going back to my house to do a few things, I'll be back later this afternoon."

Rowena walked home with one intention, to find her recliner and relax for a while. She began reading *A Long Way from Chicago*, spending the morning and afternoon engrossed. She would get up every so often to peer out the window or nibble on food.

At early evening, Rowena grabbed one of her bed pillows and went back to Mr. McGreevy's house, entering to the wonderful aroma of roast beef cooking in the oven.

Mr. McGreevy is spoiling me rotten.

After supper Rowena cleaned up the kitchen, she and Mr. McGreevy retired into the living room. He put some wood into the wood stove, and the room got toasty.

"How about we watch a movie tonight?" Mr. McGreevy suggested. "It'll get our minds off of things for a while. I'll pop some popcorn and make hot chocolate." He pulled out a dusty wooden box from a shelf full of VHS tapes.

Rowena scanned through his old movies. The selection included, *Die Hard, Lethal Weapon,* and *Dirty Harry,* all of the three *Godfather* movies among many others.

Considering my nerves are jumpy, I better pick something light hearted. Should I pick Arsenic and Old Lace, Caddy Shack or Cool Hand Luke?

Then she spotted an all-time favorite of her Grandpa's, *Silverado*.

Mr. McGreevy brought in the popcorn and hot chocolate. Rowena popped in *Silverado*. Crookie and Brengi curled up together by the warm wood burning stove.

Just as the movie got to the part where Paden takes a quick but careful aim and shoots the man off the horse, Brengi suddenly started barking.

Rowena quickly got up and turned off the TV set.

"Shush Brengi." Rowena put her index finger to her mouth. Crookie lifted his head, perked up his ears and made a mad dash under the chair. She turned the lights off in the room and together they went over to the window and peered.

Loud voices from outside filtered into the house. They could barely make out three people at the side of Rowena's house.

"I think they have someone out there," Rowena whispered.

After about fifteen minutes, there was a knock at the front door.

"Who's there?" Mr. McGreevy shouted through the door.

"It's the police. We need to speak with you."

Mr. McGreevy opened up the entrance to his home.

Chapter Twenty-two

"We believe we have caught the culprit who's been breaking into your house." The officer stepped to the side. "This is the vagrant who has been spotted around town."

Both Mr. McGreevy and Rowena looked beyond the officer. A disheveled man in handcuffs hung his head.

Rowena nearly fainted, holding onto the door jam. "That's the man I saw in the Alchemy and U the last day I talked to Patty."

"We'll be in touch with you Miss Mills. But for now, we are taking him down to the station. Please be assured he's off the streets now." Both officers led the man off and put him in a squad car.

Mr. McGreevy shut the door.

"Oh my God, that man frightened Patty," Rowena shrilled

causing Brengi to bark. "I'm sorry Brengi," She patted his head. "To think, that man broke into my house."

Mr. McGreevy took Rowena's arm and helped her to the sofa. "Maybe we should retire for the night."

Rowena tossed and turned most of the night and woke up to her phone ringing close to her ear. She sat up with a start, her mind confused from a restless sleep.

"Hello," she yawned.

"Good morning, Miss Mills, this is Officer Henry."

"Oh, yeah, hi, umm, what's up?" Rowena's senses started to sharpen.

"We've some information on the vagrant they caught last night."

"Yes? What did you find out?" Rowena's head started to throb.

"He has a rap sheet, for one thing, drug possession, and petty theft. He's a drifter, but we found his parents address. The fingerprints from your window sill match with this guy."

"Does his DNA match with the murders?" Rowena held her breath.

"It's going to be a couple of weeks, maybe three, before we get any DNA results back."

"Where do his parents live? Have they been contacted?"

"Yes, his parents have been contacted and are coming here, but it will be the day after tomorrow before they arrive."

"Why is that?"

"They live in the United States."

"What?"

"They've been looking for him for quite some time.

He has a history of mental health issues."

"That's scary."

"One thing is most troubling; we found a tablet and passport in his knapsack. The passport is stolen, of course, but when we got into his e-mails, we saw he's been communicating with you. Do you know a Rodney Luftra?"

Rowena's put her hand on her fast pulsating heart. "I've a cousin by that name. But I haven't seen him since we were children. Yes, I've been communicating with him."

"We know this has been hard on you, but could you come down to the station?"

"No, not now. I'm too stunned to do anything at this moment. Just let me know when his parents arrive. Thank you for the information, officer. Good-bye."

Rowena hit the end button on her phone.

Mr. McGreevy sat down next to Rowena. "What did the officer say?"

"The guy who broke into my house is my cousin. His parents are arriving day after tomorrow." Rowena peered aimlessly around the room.

"I'll go with you to talk to your aunt and uncle, when you are ready." He handed her a cup of hot tea.

Through blurred vision from the tears in her eyes, Rowena looked at the frail elderly man sitting next to her.

"Drink your tea, love; the hot brew will make you feel better."

Mr. McGreevy always made things better with a cup of tea.

Rowena and Mr. McGreevy drove into the village police station. Rowena parked the car and turned off the ignition, reluctant to get out.

"Come on Rowena; you can do this, I'm with you every step of the way. This has to be as hard on Rodney's parents as it is on you."

Rowena got out of the car and went around to the other side to help Mr. McGreevy out of the passenger side. He turned sideways in his seat, planting both of his feet on the ground. She handed him his cane and took ahold of his arm. After two attempts, she successfully helped hoist him out of the car. Together they shuffled into the police station.

"Good day to both of you," Officer Henry greeted. "Your aunt and uncle are in the waiting room."

Rowena paused, her nerves raw. "I don't know if I can do this."

"No worries, Miss Mills, take your time."

Rowena exhaled a deep breath—breathed slowly and looked at Mr. McGreevy. "Okay, I'm ready to conquer, hand me my sword."

Officer Henry led them to the waiting room.

Rowena stopped to assess her aunt and uncle before they walked into the waiting room.

Constance's tall height favored the Mill side of the family. She raked back a strand of her silver hair, pacing the floor while Sidney used the arms of his chair to stand. He slid his glasses up his pointed nose and held onto his stooped back.

Rowena approached her relatives. "Hello Aunt Constance, Uncle Sidney."

The couple turned around.

Rowena shook hands. "It's been a long time. This is my neighbor, Mr. Manchester McGreevy."

Mr. McGreevy offered his hand to Constance and Sidney.

"Rowena, we extend our apologies for what our son put you through," Sidney said. "A horrifying thing for Rodney to do."

Constance stood there silent.

"Rodney's Facebook page says he lives in California."

"Rodney says a lot of things. He lives with us, but when he has his episodes, it's not uncommon for him to just up and leave. He drifts around to different places. He keeps us in a state of turmoil most of the time with his erratic behavior."

Compassion welled up in Rowena.

"When Sidney and I came over here to visit Maude before she passed away, Rodney came with us. He obviously became disturbed by Maude's rejection of all of us. We certainly didn't realize how much."

Rowena's empathy temporarily escaped her. "It appears to be in the opinion of Maude's lawyer that your underhanded approach to the inheritance is the reason why she excluded you." The words flew out of her mouth, livid at Constance to say such a thing.

Mr. McGreevy shot her a surprised glance.

"Maude was getting senile." Constance wrinkled her nose as though something smelled bad.

Mr. McGreevy interjected indignantly. "It's the opinion of many, including me, that Maude had a sound mind. She, Annik, my wife, and I were neighbors for many years. You are making a false accusation."

"At this moment, I'm not going to judge the turn of events. The subject is closed as far as I'm concerned. You both have a shattered son, and this is what needs to be addressed." Rowena sighed.

Sidney's weary eyes looked down at the floor. The room screamed an awkward silence.

Constance in a snap second became fierce, resolute. "I know Rodney didn't commit those murders. As his mother, I just know."

"No, Rodney's issues run in a different type of vein. He wouldn't hurt anyone. When we heard that your mother passed away, the news set something off in Rodney. He took it upon himself with his sick mind to come and claim Maude's home." Sidney put his hands in his pocket.

"I hope you are right." Rowena softened, her sympathy returning a little.

Rowena needed to change the subject. "Aunt Constance, can you tell me anything about my dad?"

"Your father liked birds."

"My dad liked birds?"

"Yes, and dogs. Stephen always had a pigeon on his shoulder. He and the neighbor dog were the best of friends. They would dig holes together." Constance relaxed her demeanor and gave what could be described as something like a smile.

My dad liked birds. Birds and dogs.

A man walked into the waiting room and sat down.

"Mr. McGreevy and I are leaving for now. I truly hope the DNA results are in Rodney's favor. I want to believe what you told me."

Rowena and the elderly man walked down the corridor towards the door. As they passed a dark kitchen area on the right, a song from 'The Dark Side of the Moon' by Pink Floyd eerily played on the radio. ♪♪ the lunatic is in my head hahahahaha.♪♪

Inside, Officer Henry sat alone at a table. He looked up and gave them a two finger salute good-bye.

"Your aunt is a bit teasy," Mr. McGreevy offered as they drove back to his house.

"What does—teasy—mean?" Rowena queried.

"An American translation would be she's a personality like a hemorrhoid."

Rowena stifled a laugh for a moment, and then asked, "Could you tell me about your childhood?"

"My mum died when I was only five years old. My father worked at a copper mine. Being the oldest, I became the main care taker to my three younger brothers. My dad was a drunk."

"That is so sad."

"Yes, a mean drunk too. I didn't get this crooked nose playing cricket. I was fifteen when my dad died, sort of a relief."

"Oh dear, what did you and your brothers do?"

"First they put us in a residential institution and then to a working boys home. We were taught the trade of farming. We worked long hours, my brothers and me."

"I'm so sorry, Mr. McGreevy. What happened to your brothers?"

"My two brothers and I came out mostly unscathed, but my one brother became a drunkard."

Rowena pulled in the drive next to Mr. McGreevy's home.

"When my wife and I purchased this house and acreage, my farming trade came in good stead." Mr. McGreevy spanned his hand around the area. "We met your Aunt Maude at that time. Annik and I had a wonderful garden and grew luscious vegetables and herbs. Both of us became fresh fruit and vegetable growers, selling directly to retail and open markets. Did I tell you Annik and Maude were best friends? Annik loved your aunt like a sister."

Rowena looked at Mr. McGreevy, her heart aching for him, astonished at his eloquence. And his choice to be a kind human being.

Chapter Twenty-three

Simon, Daisy, and Russell pulled up in a pick-up truck, Simon backing the bed close to the front porch.

Rowena rushed out the door, held the porch railing, and stood on her toes.

"Here are your new faucets for the bathroom." Simon handed them to Rowena.

Rowena turned the shiny faucets over in her hand and admired them as if they were precious gems. "Oh my, they even have a shower attachment. And the handles sparkle."

"Rowena, this is Russell Penhall."

"Hi, Russell, it's nice to meet you."

"Morning, ma'am." Russell didn't look Rowena in the eye.

Simon and Russell unloaded Rowena's new bathtub and vanity

sink. They edged the fiberglass tub sideways through the front door and on up the stairs, then came back to take the vanity up.

Rowena tugged on her friend's ruffled sleeve and led her away from the steps and out of hearing distance. "Seriously Daisy, Russell Penhall?"

"Oh now, Rowena, nobody has been convicted of anything. Besides, Simon thinks both Harry and Russell are innocent. Simon has worked with Russell in the past and says he's a good bloke."

"I'll have to tell you all about my meeting with my Aunt Constance and Uncle Sidney." Rowena sighed. "As of now, my cousin Rodney is on the top of the suspect list. He could be a murderer. It's probable, but one should be careful."

Daisy padded Rowena on the shoulder. "Honey, that has to be weighing on your mind. Let's hope all of this gets sorted out soon."

"I haven't seen my aunt and uncle since childhood. I asked my aunt about my dad and all she could say, 'he liked birds and dogs.' That was her brother for crying out loud; wouldn't you think she could have come up with something better than that?"

"Maybe not. If everything you told me about your aunt is correct, she might not have the depth to dig any deeper into her recollections about your dad. Her fondest memories are most likely of herself."

Rowena smiled, "I think you just nailed that with a hammer."

"You have never mentioned what your dad did for a living."

"He was an English professor. That's what I set out to do before quitting school and getting married."

"An English professor," Daisy repeated. "And you know he was a smart dog and bird lover."

"I've never had the academic abilities my dad did. Sometimes I feel the fool."

"That's not true. You must have cared about your husband very much to sacrifice your education to marry him. Tell me a little about the guy."

"He sort of reminds me of Zeus, when he swallowed his pregnant first wife whole."

"Well, that particular wife was the goddess of deep thought, you know. And after he swallowed her, she became Zeus's nagging voice from within. Are you saying your ex-husband tried to squeeze the life out of you? Or that he did squeeze the life out of you and now his conscience is bothering him? And maybe your conscience is bothering you just a wee bit."

"I guess I shouldn't judge, but at this point, I wonder how much of a conscience William has. As much as he has an insatiable lust for women, I wonder if he might also have a deep seated hate for them. Still, my conscience *is* bothering me. I haven't loved William in a long while, wasting so much time confusing obsession and jealousy with love. I'm such a fool."

"We all can be foolish, at times, but you're no fool. I'm sure you gave it your best. Let me ask you this, what's your genius?" Daisy enquired ostensibly out of left field.

"What?"

"Tell me something you are really good at."

"I don't know exactly. I like to write, but that can be grueling. Once in school I got a C-on my report card in cooking class. So scratch cooking off my genius list." Rowena thought for a moment. "Could it be my intuitiveness with my choice in men?"

"Oh come on, tell me what's deep in your heart. If it makes you feel better, I will confess something I think is my genius," Daisy prodded.

"Let me see, how does that one quote go?" Rowena put her index finger to her head, and furrowed her brows to feign deep thought. "If there's anything more expensive than a college education, it's the price of ignorance. See, my brilliant mind has deducted that profound concept." Rowena held her palms up empty.

Daisy put her hands on her hips.

Rowena raised her chin at the screeching sound coming from the bathroom above. "Okay, seriously, something I might be good at—hmm, I know this is going to sound silly, but it's my dream to write a novel. Not my genius by any means, but putting ink to paper in an epic tale is something quite profound in my heart. If my dad were alive, it would please him so." Her face blushed.

"Why would I laugh? I think I've just tapped out of you something you could be good at. When the time is right, I say, go for it. The only thing you need Rowena is a little more confidence. And yes, your dad would be proud, but write for you not for him."

"Ok, your turn." Rowena tapped a finger to Daisy's chest.

"What do you mean?"

"You know what I mean." Rowena put her hands on her hips.

Oh yes, my genius. Hmmm—let me see. Getting you to admit your hidden genius." Daisy laughed.

"Honestly, I don't know what I would have done if I hadn't met you." Rowena had always been careful with who she confided in. Getting to know Daisy, she admired her integrity and felt safe. "I'm curious about you and Simon. How did you meet?"

"Actually, we met right after college, at a mutual friend's house. Simon can be rather shy, so I initiated the conversation. We had a nice chat, and I ended up asking him to a cat show with me."

"A cat show?"

"Yes, in Bristol. I know Simon must have been smitten because he doesn't particularly like cats."

Rowena and Daisy made their way to the kitchen to start lunch.

Daisy pulled out a plastic bag full of fresh vegetables from her canvas carrier. "Let's make a luscious artisan pizza for lunch."

Rowena pulled out a large pizza cooking stone.

"Your name is somewhat unusual, how did your parents come up with the name Rowena?" Daisy asked as she washed the vegetables.

"I've been told my dad admired a woman by the name of Rowena

Cade, the mastermind behind a place called the Minack Theatre. Right here in Cornwall."

"Oh yes, the Minack Theatre in Porthcurno, we've been there several times. Simon and I love the open-air theatre on a summer night." Daisy smiled. She waved the carving knife as she spoke. "The rocky granite outcrop jutting into the Atlantic Ocean," she sighed.

"My dad said Miss Cade, along with her gardener, made the terrace and seating, hauling all materials down from her house by way of a winding path from the beach below."

"Porthcurno Beach is one of the most beautiful beaches in the world. Rowena Cade was an architectural genius if there ever was one."

Rowena apprehensively looked around the room, trying to bring forth the words that were stuck in her throat. "Daisy, there's something I need to tell you, something you most likely already know—."

Outside, a car door slammed. Rowena wiped her hands on a dishtowel, went to the front door, and peered through the window. Aunt Constance and Uncle Sidney left their vehicle and headed toward the house.

Chapter Twenty-four

Rowena opened her front door as Constance and Sidney stepped onto the porch.

"Hello," Rowena greeted, "what brings you out here? Would you like to come inside?"

"No thank you," Constance said, "We can just sit out here on the porch." The wind blew a cold chill.

"Please come in, the weather is much too cold out here." Rowena offered again.

Sidney pulled out his handkerchief to wipe his cold nose as Constance lifted her scarf higher around her neck. "Only for a moment," Sidney said. They followed Rowena into the living room.

"Please, have a seat." Rowena pointed to the worn brown leather sofa.

Sidney and Constance scanned their heads around the room before sitting down. "It's been a long time since we've visited in this house," Constance said.

A tinge of sadness welled up in Rowena, mixed with a growing anxiety.

"Sorry, we came unannounced," Sidney apologized. "There's been evidence gathered that is in Rodney's favor."

"What evidence is that?" Rowena sat erect in her recliner.

"The second woman was estimated to have been killed around 1:00 am. A witness claims to have seen Rodney at the Gerard Street Pub until closing time at 2:00 am."

"I hope you're correct." Rowena pulled her hair behind her ears.

"Our only hope is that we can get Rodney back home and get him some help." Sidney appealed to Rowena.

"I know this must be most distressing for both of you."

Constance took ahold of her handbag and stood up. Sidney slowly rose and held onto his back. His looked as if his stooped shoulders carried the world on them.

The room started to fill with the aroma of freshly baking pizza. "Won't you both please stay for some lunch?" Rowena asked.

Sidney and Constance glanced at each other.

"Thanks for the offer, but we must be moving on," said Sidney.

Rowena could hear Simon and Russell coming down the stairs.

"Something sure smells good. Russell and I are famished." Simon took notice of Sidney and Constance as he spoke.

"This is my Aunt Constance and Uncle Sidney. They're just leaving."

"Hello, nice to meet you." Simon nodded.

Russell awkwardly stood in the background.

As Rowena walked behind her aunt and uncle to their rented car, she noticed fallen hairs on the back of Sidney's thread bare coat and wanted to pluck them off, in an odd sort of affectionate gesture, but stopped herself.

"I find driving a bit of a challenge over here, isn't it?" Rowena asked.

"Yes, a bit." Sidney opened his car door and slowly crawled got in.

Constance paused before getting into her side, putting her handbag by the console, then closed the door, still standing outside. She slowly walked over to where Rowena stood.

"One time when your dad was a small boy, a neighbor boy fell into a well. No adult could possibly fit into the narrow opening to help him. The rescuers came and couldn't reach him. Stephen, your dad, insisted they hoist him down the shaft. Your father saved that little boy's life."

Constance stood there another moment, pursing and relaxing her lips in a repetitive motion. She turned around and walked back to the passenger side of the car, hesitating. She looked at Rowena again, gave a slight wave, proceeded to open her door, and slipped inside.

Rowena watched as they drove off down the lane. Her eyes became moist.

Stepping back into the house, Rowena's phone rang.

The caller I.D. said it was Officer Henry.

"Hi, Officer." Rowena's heart started racing.

"Hello, Rowena."

"We've the results of the DNA test. It'd be advisable to come to the station."

Chapter Twenty-five

"Well—Mr. McGreevy, Officer Henry wants to meet with me in his office." Rowena stood at his front door. "Are you up to coming with me?"

"Of course I'm going with you young lady. Let me grab my rain shade and cane."

Mr. McGreevy and Rowena walked into the Police Station for the second time, straight into Officer Henry's office. By this time Sidney and Constance had already arrived, Rodney sitting beside them.

Rowena fidgeted with a strand of her hair, nervous. A pungent odor filled the room, the smell of strong body sweat.

Rodney peered up at Rowena, the same piercing eyes and blank gaze as before at the Alchemy and U.

Rowena's stomach dropped and she held on to Mr. McGreevy's arm, uneasy.

Officer Henry spoke first. "The DNA results do not match with Rodney's, nor do the footprints."

"We just want to get Rodney back to the States, to get him some help." Sidney's face became red, beads of sweat forming on his forehead.

Constance sat stone silent, her back erect, lower lip quivering.

"It's up to you Rowena, if you want to bring charges against Rodney with breaking and entering your home." Officer Henry shuffled papers on his desk.

Sidney and Constance looked at Rowena with pleading eyes.

"I hope you heed your parents' advice and receive help." Rowena met Rodney's eyes.

"I'm sorry if I frightened you." Rodney's voice sounded monotone. He stood up and in a swift motion, approached Rowena, attempting to hug her.

Sidney bolted up to stop him. "Rodney, please sit down." Sidney's spindly body struggled as he grabbed Rodney's arm.

Officer Henry stood up and helped Sidney put Rodney back in his seat.

Rowena's pity for Rodney and Sidney overcame her, tears welling up in her eyes. "I'll not press any charges."

Rodney looked down at the ground, rocking and hugging his own body with his arms.

"Please Rodney, get professional help, heed your parent's advice, but most important, obtain healing for yourself."

Rodney looked up at Rowena, and smiled, his teeth fuzzy and yellow.

Rowena rose from her chair and went to Mr. McGreevy, helping him to his feet. Her relatives stood up as well.

Rowena walked over to Rodney. "Good-bye, cousin." She looked at her aunt and uncle. "And good-bye to you, for now. I hope your travel back to the States is a safe one."

They both nodded. "Thank you, Rowena," Constance said. Her throat was tight and constricted.

"Officer," Rowena asked, "May I have a private moment with you, please?"

Rowena and Mr. McGreevy walked down the hall with Officer Henry.

Rowena took a deep breath, looked up at the ceiling and then back again. "Does the DNA match with anyone you know?"

"I really shouldn't say, but under the circumstances, being Simon's friend, I'll confide with you. And please don't send it any farther than this hallway."

"Of course you can confide in us, Officer."

Officer Henry looked both ways. "Some bodily fluids on Kara match with Russell Penhall. He's confessed to having sexual relations with her but swears he left about 9:00 pm."

"That's most troubling."

Mr. McGreevy stood silent, looking embarrassed by the subject matter.

"We also found some sweater fibers on her and in the bed."

"Yes?"

Officer Henry hesitated. "Um—they matched up with a sweater of Dr. Reader's."

Rowena stood still, frozen, unable to speak.

"So far however, we've not found shoes to match the prints that were at the scene of both murders. As I've mentioned to you before, a bit of mud prints were on the floor at Kara's that led to and from her bedroom window. The design goes with the soles of slick bottomed dress shoes. An odd thing it's indeed, for a scoundrel to be prowling around in a pair of those."

Rowena mind raced with the thought, *shoes can be disposed of.* "What does Harry have to say about this?" She kept her voice cool, collected.

"First of all, I don't believe for a second he is guilty, and neither would anyone else."

"I certainly don't believe he is either." But a seed of doubt started to inch its way into Rowena head.

"Harry claims Kara called him in tears after Russell left her house. He explained to me Kara took Russell's early departure as a rejection when he left right after their intimate encounter."

"I'm surprised Harry fell into that trap."

"Kara threatened suicide when she called Harry on the mobile. He went over there to calm her. He admits to having his arm around her while they sat on the edge of her bed and promised to stay until she fell asleep." Officer Henry looked from side to side, and then leaned his head in to add in a whisper, "To tell you the truth, I think Kara was a bit of a totty."

Rowena's face became hot and flushed. *Why would Kara have Harry's private mobile number?*

"Anyway, Harry claims to have left around midnight."

"Officer, would you please notify me if and when you find the culprit?"

"Of course."

Rowena and Mr. McGreevy slowly walked back to the car.

Two conflicting thoughts juxtapositoned in Rowena's mind so quickly, she wanted to scream. She made herself resolve to only one.

Someone must have come after Harry left at midnight and killed her. Yes, that must be what happened.

Chapter Twenty-six

Rowena drove Mr. McGreevy back to his house.

"Are you sure you're alright?" Rowena asked him as he opened up his side of the door.

"Yep, I've got this." He placed one foot at a time out of the car and sat for a second, holding his cane. After he raised himself up, he turned around and bent down to look into the car. "See—that was a piece of cake."

Rowena smiled, and then got somber. "I just don't know what to think of Officer Henry saying such an unkind thing about Kara. She isn't around to defend herself. And furthermore, I believe Dr. Reader is a man of integrity and if he went to Kara's house that night he went with good intentions."

Mr. McGreevy studied Rowena face. "If I didn't know better, I'd say you have a soft spot for the doctor. And as far as Officer Henry, I think he's a nice enough chap, just a small town copper, is all and a bit of a gossip. I'm stunned he's told you what he has. Still, we've not had anything like this happen in a long time around these parts. Nobody knows what to make of it or how to act."

Rowena only acknowledged the statement made about Harry. "Well—what if I *do* like Harry, it really wouldn't make any difference anyway." She looked straight ahead out the front wind shield.

"You don't have to sound defensive love; he's a good chap to be sweet on."

Rowena softened her demeanor. "To tell you the truth, I'm still not convinced my cousin Rodney wasn't the perpetrator."

"Could be, but let's hope not. Then again, every serial killer has their first victim. Perhaps it's even someone among us in the community who's snapped."

"That's a disturbing thought." Rowena exhaled.

"Yes, it certainly is. Nonetheless, as grim as I might have just sounded, please don't let bad thoughts fill that pretty little head of yours. Things have a way of working out, I promise. I'm sure sooner or later they'll find who did it."

"I hope so."

"I'm sure of it—and having said that, I think for now I'm going into the house for a lie down." Mr. McGreevy tipped his old woolen ivy cap.

"Actually, I'm not feeling well, my back aches, and I think I need to do the same."

"Yes, young lady, you've had an exhausting day. Why not take Brengi with you?"

Rowena sat in her recliner. She thumbed mindlessly through a holiday magazine filled with delicious recipes. Regardless of all the madness going on, something positive to lighten the mood in the house would be a welcome change.

I want to show them my appreciation for everything they've done. Turkey, ham, a dinner with all the essential trimmings should do the trick.

But before she planned a Christmas feast for her friends, Rowena yearned for a drive to the coast. She desired nothing more than to sit by the sea and mediate. Having been raised in the Midwest part of the States, she rarely had the opportunity to visit an ocean.

Feeling better from her rest, she promptly walked back to Mr. McGreevy's house.

"I'd like very much to go to the ocean by myself. Could I have your permission to take Brengi with me?"

The elderly gentleman watered a wilted croton plant in a ceramic pot by the entrance door.

"Yes, I think it'd do you good to get away for a spell."

Rowena laid a blanket down on the passenger side of her car, and Brengi hopped in, sat up erect, and looked straight ahead. She smiled at the dog. He seemed to understand. He's going to the ocean, riding shotgun, on the job, protecting Rowena. Life didn't get better than that. She handed him a treat. He gulped the meaty chunk with one bite.

Together, they drove the remote road to Morcant. Life is simpler in a car. The whole world momentarily shut out from everything. Rowena peered about the panoramic view of the peaceful moors. She breathed in a kinship to it all as if the air itself was part of her DNA.

A rocky peak of granite slabs appeared in the distance. Wild horses grazed below the shaded bluffs.

Mr. McGreevy had told Rowena the legendary story of the infamous yellow-eyed Black Panther 'beast' that lurked in the moors and wondered if he might be real. Or if the only true monsters were of the human kind? And did the deadly creature prowl out there at this very moment?

Rowena and Brengi passed through Morcant and continued the thirty minute drive to the ocean. She managed to find a place to park not far from the coastline. As they walked upon the lonely stretch of sand, Brengi chased a flock of little wader birds. The dog stopped in his tracks. With one paw lifted he seemed to point at the dark figure in the distance.

Shivers ran the course of Rowena's spine, as the shadow of a man grew closer. Getting closer still, his face took form—Russell Penhall—

As they came upon each other, Russell nodded.

"Hello." Rowena nodded back.

Brengi ran back to Rowena circling her and then walked beside her.

Both Russell and Rowena continued walking in opposite directions.

Rowena had an impulse to stop and look back. As she turned around to peek, Russell did so at the same time. Embarrassed, she turned back around and kept walking.

She continued her walk, and when the sheen of a seashell caught her eye, Rowena would stop to examine her find. She rubbed the smooth inner side with her fingers and gathered a select few for a coat pocket of sea treasures. Off in the distance, a lighthouse towered above the shore. As they approached the tall white structure a plank leading to the entrance opened up before them. She and Brengi walked the two hundred and fifty foot stone walkway to reach the lighthouse.

Rowena wrapped the blanket she had brought around herself for warmth and stood still for a moment, breathed in the salty air and listened to the roar of the sea. A platform encircled the perimeter of the lighthouse. They walked to the side away from the land and sat down. A fog crept in and engulfed the area. An occasional Kittiwake seagull and wary Manx shearwater would fly close by. She reached into her pocket and brought out the seashells she had collected and counted seven.

Rowena had not prayed in a long time. Not convinced she knew how, she remembered her grandmother had rosary beads that she kept on her bedroom bureau. She put the seashells in the palm of her hand and stared at them for a moment. She started touching one shell at a time, each to represent someone in her life.

The first three shells she touched were for Aunt Agnes, Uncle Robert, and Grandpa Liam.

The fourth shell for Mr. McGreevy.

The fifth shell for Daisy, Simon, Heath, and Heather.

She had two shells left. "Oh, Brengi, I can't forget you." He sidled his warm body close to her. She patted his head.

One seashell left.

Finally, she touched the last shell. "If Harry is innocent, please bring proof."

Rowena sat there at the lighthouse for almost two hours, contemplating, meditating, and wiping tears, casting her fate to the wind and the rhythmic sounds of waves.

Brengi lifted his head, alerted by something. He stood on all fours and shifted his body around toward the walking plank. He made a low growl, and then started barking.

Chapter Twenty-seven

A man's voice sounded in the still air. Rowena curled her toes into her shoes and forced her stiff legs to stand up swiftly. Brengi charged around to the other side of the lighthouse, still barking. She reached into her other pocket and held on to the mace can she had put there before the journey. She took a breath, and walked around to where Brengi stood.

A young teenage boy and his girlfriend, gazed at Brengi and Rowena, their eyes frightened, like a deer staring into headlights.

Rowena relaxed her demeanor and smiled. "Brengi, it's alright, shush boy."

The couple smiled back and the girl let out a sigh of relief as the dog quieted down. "You startled us."

"We were just leaving. Sorry, to have scared you both. Have a nice day." Rowena's reply sounded sheepish as she stroked the top of Brengis's head.

Rowena and Brengi started back toward the car. "Well, buddy, I think we upset those two, taking over their secret romantic spot."

Back at her house, Rowena rustled around in the cupboards of the sideboard, searching for necessities for the Christmas dinner. She pulled out a red linen tablecloth and matching napkins. Aunt Maude had left behind a twelve piece set of Bavarian china. They were beautifully designed with pinkish-red roses, and trimmed in silver. Tucked away in a solid cherry silverware case she found some Roger Brothers Daffodil silverware.

Rowena took on the task of washing everything, even ironing the napkins as she folded them.

Rowena got on the mobile with Daisy.

"I'm having a Christmas feast Sunday at noon and I'm giving you a heads up."

"What time do you want us there to help?' Daisy asked.

"No, seriously I've got this. One legacy my mom left me is the knowhow on preparing a Christmas feast."

"Let me at least bring something. What would you say if I brought some Yorkshire pudding?"

"Yes, that you may do." Rowena laughed "Mr. McGreevy is bringing minced pie but this is my treat."

"We'll be looking forward to coming."

"See all of you Sunday. Bye."

"Yes, we'll be there with bells on. Bye."

The evening before the dinner, Rowena put the extending leaf into the mahogany table in the dining room, spreading the festive tablecloth over it, smoothing the linen with her hands. She then set the table, placing the crystal goblets to the left of each setting. She kept straightening everything to perfection, even lining the chairs up. *Have I forgotten anything?*

She read and reread the recipes. She replayed in her mind on how to coordinate the timing just right.

She stuffed the turkey and placed it in the oven at a low temperature to slow cook through the night.

Rowena lay on the sofa that night, rehearsing the words she wanted to say to everyone in her toast. She became restless when her back muscles started to spasm, and then subside.

Going into the kitchen to make a cup of warm milk, she returned to the living room and relaxed in the recliner. She then picked up a book to read until she became sleepy. Starting to doze, she heard the screech owl outside the front window, trilling and whistling again. *That's a good omen.*

She fell asleep peacefully and awoke at the beginning of dawn to the wonderful aroma of roasting turkey.

As she rose, her lower back still ached, and she braced it with her hands.

Just get me through the day.

Chapter Twenty-eight

Rowena stretched her back and turned side to side; she then opened the blinds that gave a view of the front porch. A familiar tail wagged from outside.

"Hi Brengi, have you been sitting by my front door looking out for me?" She patted him on his head. "You're a good boy. Come on in while I fuss around in the kitchen. You don't have to give me those puppy eyes; I'll get you a treat."

Brengi followed Rowena to the entrance of the kitchen and sat down. With his long nose lifted, he whiffed the scent of the turkey cooking.

Rowena opened up the oven and basted the bird and with a fork peeled off a bit of the meat. She blew until the curling steam went away. "Here ya go." She tossed the dog the piece and he caught it in his mouth. "I'm going to be busy in here for a while. Feel free to make yourself at home." She smiled.

Everyone arrived at the same time. Mr. McGreevy brought into the kitchen his fresh baked mince pies and Daisy followed behind with her Yorkshire pudding. Heath and Heather came in after their mother with rosy cheeks from the cold.

"Do you mind if I help you carve the turkey? That's one of my specialties." Mr. McGreevy already had the carving knife in his hand.

"One of your many talents, I'm sure. Be my guest." Rowena moved to the side to let him start slicing away.

Rowena started bringing in the dishes and putting them on the buffet table. In the center of the set dining table, Daisy had placed a poinsettia plant.

"Thank you, what a lovely finishing touch that brings."

"You're quite welcome." Daisy helped carry in more dishes.

Rowena filled everybody's goblets with sparkling water. "I think everything is ready now." She stood back and gave the prepared table a nod. "You can take your place at the table."

The kids raced up to choose a seat and everyone sat down.

"Before we start filling our plates, I want to give my thanks."

All eyes looked at Rowena as she stood up.

"I've prepared this meal in my appreciation of each and every one of you. I'm so blessed to have a gathering of friends I've grown to care about deeply. All of you in your own way have brought me into a different emotional universe."

"Mr. McGreevy, you appeared one day to introduce yourself to me. You couldn't have known that I was going through one of the darkest moments of my life. You nourished my body with your delicious stews and healed my heart and soul with your kind words and wisdom. You've been like an angel to me. Call it serendipity; I know you were put right in my path. I'd fallen from a cliff of regret and hung on the edge of disparity when you came along and lifted me up. You helped save me, my dear friend." Rowena's eyes had been downcast and when she looked up at Mr. McGreevy, his sweet clouded eyes were filled with tears.

"To my new friends, Simon, Daisy, Heath and Heather—this home is filled with smiles and laughter because of you. It wouldn't have been possible for me alone to transform this sad little house into a warm and lovely dwelling, such as it is now. Because when I first arrived, I hadn't enough will left in me to move forward alone. But you have shown me what true love really is. I've enough money for counsel taxes and various fees. I'm making an offer to you, in gratitude; to have you all live in this home for as long as you want to. I'll visit here every year. Could you help me fix up the attic as my living quarters? That enclosed room would be a perfect writing room. That's of course if you would want to live here."

Between their empty plates, Simon reached for Daisy's hand

without taking his eyes away from Rowena. Heath and Heather looked at each other with wide open eyes.

Then Simon spoke up. "We have some good news of our own. I just got word I'm going back to work." He looked at his wife as she smiled and nodded. "Still, we'd be honored to live here, but only if we pay our fair share"

Rowena lifted her glass.

Everyone else stood up and lifted their glasses.

"I toast my good friends and their good fortune."

"Hear, hear."

After the meal, Rowena excused herself and went to the kitchen. That same strange feeling crept up her back. By the sink, the uncomfortable sensation turned to pain, and she grabbed unto the counter top. She looked down at the floor and she was standing in a pool of water.

The aching became so intense, Rowena cried out.

Daisy rushed in. "Oh dear," Daisy said as she put one arm around Rowena and clutched her arm with the other. "Simon, please come in here and help me. But first call Dr. Reader, now!"

Chapter Twenty-nine

Simon ran into the kitchen holding his cell phone. Rowena listened as Simon spoke into the phone. "Can you please come out to Morwen Cottage? Rowena needs help right away."

"Yes? What did he say?" Daisy kept her voice calm.

"He's going to be a while—um, he's an hour away." Simon stammered.

He and Daisy got Rowena up the stairs and onto her bed.

Mr. McGreevy followed behind them, holding onto the railing. "You'll be alright, honey. We're here with you."

Daisy went over to the vanity and grabbed a ponytail holder and twisted her hair up tight in a bun. She ran into the bathroom to wash her hands, coming back into the room, wiping them with a towel. "Why didn't you tell me you were this far along?"

"I'm not! I still have another month to go. My plans were to have this baby in the States." Rowena cried in pain. She looked down at her swollen belly. "Not in Cornwall!" She kicked away her pants under the sheets.

"Well, love, this baby seems to have a mind of its own and wants to be born a Brit. It doesn't look like this little tyke is even going to wait for Dr. Reader." Daisy sat down next to Rowena and took her hand.

Dr. Reader! Rowena cringed again and tears glossed over her eyes. Her addled mind went strange, distorted. She wanted to scream out terrible things about him. She bit her tongue. A drop of blood trickled down her chin.

Daisy ran into the bathroom and moistened a washrag and rolled it up. She handed it to Rowena. "Bite into this when the pains come."

Rowena wanted to jump up and run out of the room. "Please make the pain stop."

"When did your labor first start?" Daisy looked beneath Rowena's covers.

"I'm not sure. My back ached last night and this morning." Another pain came, and she screamed out. "I want my mother. Please, someone, get my mother."

"I think you've been in labor a while. The baby has crowned and thankfully in proper position. Everything is going to be alright, Rowena."

Rowena pushed and groaned, her body drenched with sweat.

"Push a little more; I can see some dark hair. Come on, you're doing great, just breathe." Simon placed clean towels and scissors beside her. He blew out air from his lungs as though he too experienced pain.

Mr. McGreevy remained in the corner of the room with his eyes bulging.

Rowena looked feverishly up at Simon and Mr. McGreevy. "Both of you out of here!"

They both bolted out of the room.

Rowena's pain subsided for a moment. "I'm so sorry. Please come back in. Just don't look at me."

Both Simon and Mr. McGreevy reappeared by the opening of the bedroom door, peeking inside, and then entering, diverting their eyes. Simon paced as the elderly man went back to his corner.

Rowena let out a long agonizing scream. She thought her insides were ripping apart.

And then the pain disappeared.

Is that a whimper I hear? Crying? A baby is crying? What is Daisy saying?

"What a sweet little girl you are. You're such a tiny little thing. Oh, but so strong and healthy, yes you are." Daisy spoke to the baby as she laid her on a clean towel and cut the cord.

Rowena lay on the bed, sheets soaking wet. "Did you say a little girl? She's alright?"

"Oh yes, she's quite alright, delicate, like a little violet." Daisy cooed as she sponged the baby off.

Simon ran downstairs and brought back with him an old kitchen scale and placed it on the bureau.

Daisy put down a clean flour sack towel and then gently laid the baby on it. "5 pounds and 6 ounces she is. And born at 4pm on Christmas Eve."

Daisy gently propped up pillows under Rowena's head, and then placed the baby in her arms.

"Thank you, Daisy. How can I ever thank you?" Rowena's voice sounded weak.

Daisy leaned down and kissed Rowena on the forehead. "We did good."

Simon and Mr. McGreevy came to the bedside to see the baby.

Mr. McGreevy patted Rowena on the head, beaming. "She's a lovely baby."

"Yes, quite a cute little thing." Simon smiled.

Rowena looked over at the bedroom door and saw Dr. Reader's silhouette standing in the doorway.

In her primeval receptive state of mind, Rowena imagined him a tall and handsome angel...

Still half asleep, Rowena glanced over at the clock on the night stand; it read 6:00 am.

The baby stirred and then cried tiny peeps like a little bird. *She must be hungry.*

Rowena swung her legs around and sat up at the side of the bed. The baby lay in a makeshift crib beside her in a dresser drawer.

Daisy came into the bedroom. She'd spent the night, sleeping in the room across the hall, helping throughout the late hours. She went over and smiled down at the fussing infant, then picked her up, smiling. "Good morning sweetie. Happy Christmas." She looked up at Rowena. "You look a bit exhausted." She handed the hungry baby to Rowena. "I'll just be down in the kitchen."

Rowena nodded.

With the baby's tummy full and burped, Rowena lay on her side and propped her head with her elbow. She played with the baby's fingers and toes, fascinated by her beauty. "Hi there, my little one, what in the world should I name you?"

What will William do when he finds out about her? Certainly he'll want her in his life. What will his mother have to say about it? I'll just have to deal with that when the time comes.

She lightly touched the tip of the baby's nose and whispered, "I'd lasso the moon for you, sweetie. And your grandma Ingrid would be so proud of you."

She heard a light knock on the door.

"How's mummy and baby doing?" Mr. McGreevy opened the

door and shuffled in carrying a breakfast sandwich wrapped in a kitchen napkin.

"That's so kind of you." Rowena sat up in the bed.

Mr. McGreevy put the sandwich on her lap.

"Did you sleep well downstairs on the sofa?"

He went over and sat on the opposite side of the bed. "Yes, I did alright. I hope you don't mind. I slept on your recliner."

"I'll move the baby and myself downstairs so you won't have to climb the stairs."

"She's a lovely baby Rowena." Have you thought of a name for her?"

"Not for sure yet. I've a couple of names wrestling around in my head."

Rowena's cell phone made a chiming noise indicating a text.

Dr. Reader. *"I'll stop by around 3:00 to check on the baby and you."*

Rowena put the phone down. "Harry is stopping by around 3:00 to check on everything." She took a whiff of the egg biscuit and pulled back the foil on her orange juice cup. "You are so good to me, Mr. McGreevy."

Daisy entered the room. "I can stay until about 1:00. We're having a Christmas dinner at Simon's sister. You look to be good hands with Mr. McGreevy. Then I'll be back tomorrow morning." She laid down a dozen folded flour sack towels. "And I'll bring some baby nappies and necessities. Until then, these kitchen clothes will have to do."

"Thank you. That'd be so nice. I've went through most of the clean pillowcases diapering."

"I've washed them out already. They are currently hanging near the kitchen fireplace to dry."

As she sat in the chair nursing the baby, Rowena heard a car pull up. Sounds of rustling and the front door opening and closing made its way upstairs.

It seemed a long time before Harry came up to the room, rapping on the door jamb. "Hi, how are you both doing?"

"The baby is doing well." Rowena smiled.

"When she's finished nursing, I'll check her vitals and weight." He set his doctors bag on the night stand.

"She's just finishing up." The baby made a loud burp and they laughed.

Harry used great care in lifting the child out of Rowena's arms and they shared a look.

Rowena followed them and lowered her hips onto the bed.

Harry opened his bag and first brought out a canvas sack. "Earlier today I had Christmas dinner with Donna, my nurse and her family. She gathered a few things from her grandkids to give you until you can shop properly." He handed the bag to Rowena.

"Oh—how thoughtful. Please tell Donna thank you for me until I'm up and about to do it myself." She undid the gift and found four clean onesies and a half a dozen nappies.

Harry brought out a stethoscope and thermometer and examined the baby. "She *is* doing quite well, yes. She's a bit tiny, so keep her warm, and maybe hold her by a window that gets plenty of sunshine. How're you feeling? You look healthy enough."

Rowena rolled her eyes. "Gee, thanks." She snickered.

From outside came a sputtering noise and then a loud backfire, followed by a tic-tic-tic sound, similar to a small tractor engine. Rowena lifted herself up from the bed and peered out the window.

Going down the lane was Mr. McGreevy in his 1963 green Morris Minor, a cloud of black smoke trailed behind in the evening dusk.

"I wonder where in the world he's going to." Rowena stared wide eyed back at Harry.

He took the stethoscope from his ears. "The old chap is running into the village to try and find a shop open to buy some nappies. I told him everything would be closed but I see he snuck out anyway." Harry grinned back at Rowena.

"Aww…are you serious? I could have at least loaned him my car. He must not like rinsing out diapers in the toilet." Rowena laughed. "Ouch, that hurt." She held her side and gently sat back on the bed.

"Take it easy there, mummy." Harry chuckled— then hesitated

before he spoke again. "You put yourself and the baby at risk. You should have been more prepared and sought medical attention."

Rowena watched Harry's eyes. "I've been slipping off to Truro once a week to see a nurse's practitioner. I wouldn't have let anything happen to this little girl. My plans were to travel back to the states to have the baby."

Harry smiled. He lightly pushed a fallen strand of Rowena's hair away from her face. "May I ask how old you are?"

"I'm thirty-one."

His fluid, dilated eyes came back to hers. "It's kind of Mr. McGreevy to stay with you but I think you need a nurse to help you for a while. I can make arrangements."

"I don't want to leave Mr. McGreevy out here all alone. Besides, Daisy is going to come out here daily to help me. We'll be fine. I do appreciate your offer though."

"Well, at least let me help you both down stairs. I have a gift." Harry picked the baby up, took Rowena's arm and walked with them down to the first floor.

As they reached the living room, Rowena spotted the baby crib Harry had assembled.

"Harry, thank you so much. This is indeed a Happy Christmas. Won't you please stay for a bit?"

Harry sat down on the sofa and looked around at the room. "This place sure has shaped up nicely."

"Yes, I can't tell you how I appreciate—."

Rowena stopped mid-sentence. The tic-tic-tic sound of the Morris Minor came back up the lane, and then silence. Mr. McGreevy's footsteps landed on the porch, followed by the sound of rustling keys. Harry briskly got up and opened the front door.

As Mr. McGreevy started through the door, he held a large package of newborn nappies. "I went to a friend's house and convinced him to open up his shop long enough to purchase these."

Harry took them out of his arms.

Rowena gave Harry a gentle hug before he left and as she opened the door to say good-bye, Mr. McGreevy walked in carrying a plastic container full of leftovers.

"Here doctor, I've prepared some food for you to take home. Rowena put on quite the feast."

"Why thank you, Manchester. That's thoughtful of you. I look forward to tasting Rowena's fine cuisine." He winked at her.

"Good evening, Doctor." The older gentleman nodded a farewell to Harry.

After she closed the door, Rowena narrowed her eyes and put her hands on her hips. "If I didn't know better, I'd say you were trying to trick Harry into thinking I'm a good cook."

"Well—maybe a bit, but it's all for the good cause."

"For the *what?*" Rowena laughed. "You're really something, you know that?"

As Mr. McGreevy walked to the couch with a book in his hand, he answered over his shoulder, "Right back at ya, kid."

Rowena glanced down at the package of diapers and her face blushed pink when she spotted another small box right beside it—feminine pads. *The kind shop owner must have brought this issue to his attention. Aargh.*

Mr. McGreevy continued to read into the evening hours.

"I see you're reading Mark Twain." Rowena sat down in the recliner across from him with the baby asleep in her arms.

"This one is, *Life on the Mississippi*. I've read and reread most of his stories. I never tire of the adventures. I've always dreamed of going to the mighty river. But I've traveled there many times through his books."

"I think I mentioned to you I was raised in the area not far from *Tom Sawyers* birth place."

Mr. McGreevy put the book down. "I'm going to miss you when you go back."

"I'm going to miss you too." A thought came to her like a bolt of lightning. "Why don't you come back with me? I mean to the States. The airlines are quite accommodating to seniors."

"You know, that's a thought. The worst that could happen to me is keeling over from utter happiness."

"I can take you to the area where Mark Twain's stories took place; we'll ride on an old riverboat and dine in themed restaurants."

Mr. McGreevy sat in his chair smiling. "Simon and Daisy could take care of Brengi and Crookie." His voice became animated. "That'd be a dream come true."

"I'll make all the arrangements. My Aunt Agnes and Uncle Robert would love to accommodate you. And you and my grandpa will hit it off, I'm certain of it. Did I mention in his prime he was a Middle Weight Boxing Champ? He had a mean left hook."

"You don't say? I like your grandpa already."

"Plus, you'll have to be with me to witness the expression on my aunt's face when I waltz through customs at the airport carrying a baby. That'll be priceless."

"Not to mention dragging a ninety-year-old man with you." Mr. McGreevy smiled and then looked at the clock. "Will you look at the time? It's nearly 10 o'clock. This old chap needs his beauty sleep. Good night, lovely."

"Good night, my friend."

Rowena went to shut off most of the lights and double checked all the locks. When she returned to the living room, Mr. McGreevy was asleep and snoring. She covered him with a blanket and gently removed his crooked eyeglasses.

She leaned down at the new crib and kissed her sleeping angel's forehead.

Rowena slept sporadically in her recliner, the baby waking twice in the night to be fed.

At the break of dawn, Rowena woke up to Mr. McGreevy stirring in the kitchen and the smell of bacon and eggs cooking, blended with fresh brewed coffee. She lay there, savoring the moment of silence and the wonderful aromas. In the crib next to her, the baby took a deep breath and exhaled.

She heard a crashing sound and sat straight up in her recliner. It was the sound of plates and glasses falling to the floor.

"Mr. McGreevy!"

Chapter Thirty

Rowena ran to the kitchen.

Mr. McGreevy lay sprawled on the floor, plates and food scattered everywhere.

Rowena knelt down next to him, trying to feel for a pulse. Unable to sense one, she turned him on his back. He looked so frail she feared his bones would break if she gave him CPR. But she started pumping his chest, gently, refusing to stop. She kept the momentum up and continued breathing into his mouth. As her strength began to dissipate, she paused for a moment to look at him. His eyes were open, staring at nothing. "Please, Mr. McGreevy, don't give up." She cried.

Rowena pumped his chest again and again and tried to breathe her own life into his. "Wake up! Don't you dare die on me!" She stopped from exhaustion, her head falling on his chest. Her wailing started at first quietly, deep within her soul and then made its way out of her mouth.

An indiscernible amount of time passed before she slowly got up to find her phone.

Rowena couldn't remember how to use her mobile. *God, help me!* Her hands shook so severely, nothing but random numbers appeared on the keypad. Her head pounding, she cleared everything, breathed, and found Harry's text. She touched the green phone icon.

The baby stirred and started fussing.

"Please, don't cry, not now."

She listened to the ringing. *Answer, answer, answer.*

"Hello, Rowena."

Her voice got caught in her throat.

"Hello. Is this an emergency? Please speak up."

"It's me, Rowena." Her voice, nothing but a hoarse whisper.

"Mr. McGreevy is dead. Please help me."

Honoring Manchester McGreevy's wishes, he was cremated and laid to rest in the Urn Garden outside of Morcant beside his beloved Annik. Many from the village attended the memorial and gave warm homilies. Two of his brothers were present and several nieces and nephews from both his and Annik's family.

Morwen Cottage

"For now, we'll bring his pets into town to stay with us at the manor." Daisy whispered to Rowena as they stood at the ceremony.

Rowena listened in silence.

"Rest assured, Simon, and I'll be moving into Morwen Cottage in the late spring after school lets out. They'll become our own." Daisy stroked the back of Rowena's shoulder.

When the memorial finished, Rowena walked over and put a wreath of wild flowers by the Manchester and Annik McGreevy urns, kneeling down. "Good-bye, my dear friend. You're now with your beloved wife." She lightly touched both of their urns.

Simon and Daisy stood in silence behind Rowena and then walked with her back to the car.

"You won't be able to stay out at the cottage alone with the baby," Daisy said. "Both of you can stay with us at the large manor in the village until you go back to the States. Simon's sister Jesse and her husband have plenty of room. They already know you're coming and welcome you."

"Thank you. That's most kind of all of you. Today is the second of January, if everything goes as planned, I'll leave the first of February to go back home."

Simon, Daisy, Rowena, and the baby went back to the cottage to gather up some things.

"Would you mind if I went over to Mr. McGreevy's house alone to feed and visit Brengi and Crookie?"

"Of, course, take all the time you need." Simon took the infant from her arms.

She unlocked and entered the front door. Where Brengi would've greeted her, tail wagging, he just lay curled up by the unlit hearth, looking up with sad eyes. She went over to him and stroked his back. "Come on boy, let's go outside for a bit."

Brengi reluctantly got up and followed Rowena outside.

Coming back in, Crookie made his appearance, his eyes watery and matted from stress. He came over and brushed up against her.

Rowena sat on the floor, leaning her back against the sofa as Crookie jumped on her lap and she petted him. Brengi slowly sidled up to her and lay down. His tail curled down between his legs. Tears flowed down her face and dripped onto Crookie. With a constricted voice she spoke to them. "There, there boys, I know how awful this is for you. I promise with all my heart we'll take good care of you."

After an imperceptible amount of time Daisy walked through the front door to get her.

Rowena stood up and had dried tears on her cheeks. Daisy gently brushed them off with her thumb.

"I think I've decided what I'm going to name my baby."

Chapter Thirty-one

"Here, put this on. It'll help cover your tummy," Daisy said. She laid a silver lame skirt and long black tunic on the bed. "And dab some color to your lips and cheeks. You and I are dragging Simon to the Alchemy tonight for Karaoke. You haven't lived until you've heard Simon sing. It's been three weeks since you've had the baby and a night out will do you some good."

Rowena looked at Daisy with a bit of apprehension.

"Now don't look so worried, Daisy smiled. "Jesse has already volunteered to babysit and a night of fun has been arranged. Your baby will be fine. We're leaving in an hour. Be ready."

Rowena slipped into the skirt and blouse Daisy handed her. She sat down at the dressing table and opened up her cosmetic container and peered inside at her make-up. Not having worn anything on her face in months, she fished around trying to find the right colors. Applying eye make-up first, she finished off with a blush lipstick and then opted to wear her long hair down.

"This is as good as it's going to get." Rowena shrugged at her reflection and went downstairs to check the baby's supply of milk for the evening.

"Will you look at Simon? Isn't he debonair tonight? Jesse commented as Simon entered the kitchen.

"I don't think I've ever seen you so spruced up Simon." Rowena smiled as she put on her coat.

"Yes, he always dresses up fit to kill when he gets together with his cronies to sing and cut the rug." Daisy eyed Simon with an expression of admiration. "And will you look at that, you've even shined your shoes."

They hopped in Simon's SUV for the short drive to the Alchemy and U. As they entered the establishment, the darkness of the pub contrasted beautifully with the white string lights draped throughout the ceiling. The music had a crowd of people dancing on the makeshift dance floor to the festive rhythm.

"Over there, quick, I think there's a table with four chairs." Simon gestured to the empty seats.

After Rowena sat down, she scanned the room. Next to them, a guy slouched in his chair as his date searched her cellphone and ignored him. At another table, girls raised shot glasses in a group toast and laughed.

Different ones were taking turns getting up on stage singing, some good, and others comically off key.

A waitress placed a plate of appetizers on the table. "What'd you like to drink?" She asked.

"I'd like a white wine, please," Rowena said.

"My wife and I'll have two brown ales, thanks."

Three guys came over to the table. "Well, Simon, you ready to pop-off a song or two?" The one with jeans and t-shirt asked with an accent of strong British flare. The two other guys had on balder bibs with crusher hats. They had a slight smell about them.

Daisy leaned over and spoke above the music into Rowena's ear. "Those two guys are fishermen who come in on Wednesday nights for karaoke. Don't let their appearance throw you, those four sing in a quartet that'll dissolve your heart into mush. The one guy, the taller one, Big Willie, he can also sing the blues, and I don't mean maybe."

Simon got up and made his way to the stage with his three friends. On point, the music for, *Cry For Me*, started up and Simon began in a tenor voice with a perfect vibrato, his cohorts harmonizing to the melody.

Sitting in her chair, Rowena's jaw dropped. She became mesmerized, the music hypnotizing. When they finished the song, Rowena forgot herself, and let out a loud whistle, she then yelled. "More!"

Daisy looked over at Rowena and started laughing.

Something stirred in Rowena, and she made her way to the stage.

As Simon and his friends walked off, she went to them. "Bravo guys. That was beautiful. I want to hear more." She continued onto the stage, possessed in the spirit of fun, her ham bone long repressed. *What do I have to lose? The worst thing to happen would be total embarrassment and humiliation.* "Do you have, *I Can't Give You Anything But Love?*" She asked through the microphone to the guy in charge of the music.

The music man signaled an O with his thumb and index finger and winked one eye.

So in her soft mezzo-soprano voice, Rowena gave it her all and sang her heart out. She noticed people sitting around the place, looking up smiling. And then—*oh dear,* Harry walked through the front door of the pub and made his way to sit down with Simon and Daisy. He looked up at Rowena, giving his full attention. When the song finished, the people clapped, some whistled.

"That was lovely. You never mentioned you could sing." Daisy praised as Rowena sat back down and nodded at Harry.

"Thank you so much. It's been years. I'm quite rusty. Well—I didn't know Simon could sing either. I guess we learn something new about each other every day."

Three more people took their turn in singing. And then a fourth song, a slow one, *We Are All Alone,* started to play.

Harry looked at Rowena. Would you like to dance?"

Rowena hesitated. "I don't know Harry; I haven't danced in a long time."

"It's a slow dance, what could go wrong?" Harry asked.

Daisy shot Rowena a side glance and pointed with her eyes towards to dance floor.

I'm beginning to think Daisy and Simon set this whole thing up.

Harry stood up and took Rowena's hand and led her to the dance floor. He put his arm around the small of her back and took her hand.

A sensation filled Rowena's body, dreamlike and foreign to her, and she never wanted to stop holding his broad shoulders. She could smell the sweet scent of mint on his breath as she rested her head on his chest, listening to his heart beat. *Are all hearts this beautiful?* They danced until the Deejay took a break.

Rowena took her head off of Harry's shoulder and smiled up at him.

"Thank you, Rowena," Harry said in a soft voice. He followed her back to the table, his hand still on the arch of her back as if he didn't want to let go of her."

"I know I sound like a kill joy, but I must get back to the baby." Rowena picked up her hand bag and peeked at her mobile.

"It's a mild night tonight. Why don't you let me walk you back home, it isn't more than a couple of blocks?" Harry offered.

"Thank you, yes, I'd like that Harry. I hope you two don't mind that I'm leaving."

Simon and Daisy looked at each other and smiled. "No, enjoy your walk," Daisy said.

Coming from the noisy pub, outside in the night air, the stillness and quiet engulfed them, their breath steaming.

As they approached the brick Victorian Manor, the elegant home radiated a beautiful glow with its gas lights lining the cobblestone walkway leading to a covered veranda. Jesse and her husband, Curtis, had turned the place into a Bed and Breakfast.

As magical as the night was, something now held her back, an indescribable sense of doom. *Why can't I shake Officer Henry's words he spoke that day at the police station?*

She'd promised him confidentiality, and would forever honor that promise, but her profound curiosity about Harry's relationship with Kara had brought a constant gnawing at her wellbeing.

"I've had a wonderful night with you, Rowena. There's something about you that reminds me of your Aunt Maude. And I mean that in the nicest sense of the word." Harry took Rowena's hand in his.

The touch of his hand momentarily thrilled her and she looked up at Harry as they walked.

Harry brought his gaze back to her. "You're so beautiful." He squeezed her hand.

"I'm fortunate to have met you. I can't believe how much my life has changed in only a year. Not long ago, I lived like a racing train on a track ready to derail. But when I felt I couldn't hang on any longer, that's just when the tide turned for me."

"Simon has filled me in on some of your life. I'd say you remind me of a Phoenix, one who has burst into flames and then been reborn from the ashes."

"Oh Harry, do you really think that? I like the poetry in your words. Hmm—a Phoenix, I'll own that one. And thank you for seeing me as a symbol of strength. It's quite flattering."

They approached the front steps and started walking up them. Harry stopped and stood on the one below Rowena. He turned her around so they were eye to eye. Without a word, he put his arms around her waist.

In anticipation of what would come, Rowena put her arms around his neck, stroking his upper back; the softness of his beige cashmere overcoat electrified her senses.

He kissed her lightly on the lips.

"May I ask you a question?" Rowena hid her worried frown with her fingertips and blinked her eyes.

"Of course, ask me anything." He lightly kissed her cheek.

"Did you have a relationship with Kara?" Rowena hated to spoil the moment, but something in her had to know and she refused to build another relationship on lies.

Harry's body tensed up and released his arms from around her. "To tell you the truth, that's none of your business." He exhaled. "I see you've formed an opinion of things."

"I haven't, I promise. I'm so sorry to have asked. I just thought that day in the restaurant she appeared jealous of your attentions to me."

Harry was quiet a moment. "Well—a guy gets lonely once in a while."

"Yes, of course. You knew her before I even made an appearance here."

Harry slowly backed away, taking both of her hands. "Good bye, Rowena. I've had a wonderful time tonight. I guess I'll see you and the baby at her next appointment." He released her hands, turned around and left into the night.

Why would I sabotage a perfect moment like that? I know he's innocent, don't I? Rowena's chest ached with sadness as Harry walked away.

Into the darkness Harry strode, wounded. He knew a seed had been planted in the minds of the people of the village. He had fallen hopelessly in love with Rowena, and she has just given away her true feelings.

How can one hurt so profoundly and live on. He knew he'd never be able to shake the shroud of doubt against him. He'd rather give up on love than be with Rowena and have her believe this dark shadow hanging over him.

I'd rather disappear forever than stay in Morcant if I thought even one person believed I'd do such a thing.

Chapter Thirty-two

Rowena laid the borrowed skirt and blouse across a chair and then plopped on the bed with a huff. She covered her face with her hands and peeked between her fingers at her cell phone. She grabbed the device, searched for Harry's number, and hesitated. With a second thought, she tossed the electronic temptation into her open suitcase. "You chicken," she whispered to herself.

"Knock, knock," Jesse said as she rapped on her door.

"Just a second." Rowena stood up and put a terry robe on. She tried to compose herself. "Come on in."

Jesse came in holding the sleeping baby and gently put her in the crib. "Did you have a good time?"

"Yes, we had a lot of fun. Simon is quite the singer and entertainer." Rowena tried to sound light hearted.

"I see you've packed some of your things."

"Yes, I better do a little at a time, I'm leaving with a lot more than I came with." Rowena looked around the room at all the baby things.

Daisy popped her head in the door. "I wanted to check and make sure you made it home safe. I hope you had a good time tonight."

"Oh, yes, I had a wonderful time." Rowena sniffed. She found back her tears, but heat rose to her cheeks and around her swollen eyes.

"I'll see you in the morning." Jesse went to leave the room.

"Good night, Jesse. Thanks so much for your help."

Daisy came in. "What's wrong?"

"Nothing."

Daisy came over to Rowena. "Don't tell me that. It looks as though your heart is breaking"

"I'm just miserable about leaving. I'm going to miss you and Simon and the kids. And I'm so sad about Mr. McGreevy." Rowena took a deep breath.

"And...Harry?" Daisy asked

Rowena couldn't bear to speak about how she'd lost him too. She peered up at Daisy with tears rolling down her face, leaving streaks from her make-up. She wiped them with the sleeve of her robe. "I just wish the authorities would find who did those awful murders." Her voice was constricted.

Daisy put her arms around Rowena. "I know, we all hope for that."

The baby stirred around and started to cry with hunger. Rowena picked her up and took her to the cushioned rocker chair by the bed to nurse her.

"I'll see you in the morning." Daisy left Rowena to the stillness of her room.

"Goodnight, Daisy."

After the baby drank her fill and had fallen back asleep in the crib, Rowena laid there in total darkness and she thought to herself. *What it boils downs to be: either I have a mad crush on the sweetest, kindest man in Morcant, or I've fallen for a psychopathic nut.*

Rowena buckled up the baby to take her for her last doctor's examination before returning to the states. She hadn't seen nor heard from Harry since that night he walked her home. She stuck a piece of gum in her mouth to help the butterflies in her stomach. As she found a parking spot right in front, she inhaled slowly and exhaled. *You can do this.*

"Hi Rowena, the doctor will be with you both shortly," The reception nurse, Donna said as she held out forms connected to a clipboard. "Could you fill these out, please?"

After about ten minutes, a patient came through from the examining area and went to grab his coat and hat.

Harry appeared at the door of the waiting room. "I've got this one," Harry said to Donna. He turned to Rowena and stared at her, his eyes blood shot. "I can see you now." His Adams apple moved up and down his throat as though he swallowed hard, but he didn't look away until he and Rowena stood close in the small hallway.

After a few breaths, Rowena held up her paperwork.

"Annik Manchester? Harry looked at the charts, then at Rowena.

"Yes, but I think I'll call her Mannie." Rowena took the blanket off the baby as they made their way to an examining room.

"I like that name. It suits her." Harry picked up Mannie and laid her on the baby scale. "Oh yes— she is putting on weight."

"She does eat well." Rowena kept her eyes on the baby as he measured her length and wrote down the numbers.

"I can see that." He listened to her heart with the stethoscope.

Rowena became lost in his sad, soft brown eyes until Mannie kicked her chubby legs and squealed. They laughed together for a moment.

"Mannie and I are leaving day after tomorrow." Rowena proclaimed abruptly.

Harry stopped smiling. He held Rowena in his gaze and nodded. "I'm going out of town for a couple of days to a little village near Exeter."

Rowena bit her bottom lip. "You're leaving? A vacation?"

"Perhaps I'm going for business reasons too. I've been thinking about taking a job there."

Morwen Cottage

"No! You can't. I mean… This village would be lost without you." Sadness welled up in Rowena.

Harry only nodded and gathered a tray with the HepB immunization shot for Mannie. The baby wasn't the only person who wanted to cry during the injection.

Rowena comforted her little girl by wrapping the baby back in her blanket. She held her child close to her pounding heart. "It'll be okay, sweetheart." She rocked Mannie and wanted to repeat those same words to herself.

Harry ran a gentle hand across the curly hairs on the back of Mannie's head. Close to Rowena, he spoke in a soft voice. "Whether I continue my work here or choose to move, I think it's best if we say good-bye now. May I walk you and Mannie to your car?"

Rowena gave a nod and waited for him to finish filling out Mannie's shot records. When she held out her hand to shake his, he hesitated in releasing it. He then handed her the immunization papers. "Here, you'll need this when Mannie has her two month check-up."

"You look at bit pale. Are you feeling alright?" she asked. Rowena wanted to hug him but stopped herself short, instead she touched his arm.

Harry didn't respond to Rowena's comment but looked at where her hand laid on him.

"Thank you for everything Harry. I hope to see you when we come back." She laid Mannie in her carrier.

Harry took both of her hands in his and stared at them for a moment and then looked up into her eyes. "You have a beautiful little daughter. I hope the very best to both of you."

"I appreciate that. We will try our best."

Harry lifted the baby carrier and walked with her to the door.

Rowena waved good-bye to Donna.

"Safe travels. I hope to see you again, soon."

Rowena nodded. "Thanks."

Harry walked them to the car and he secured the baby in her seat. He went around and opened Rowena's door, then turned her towards him. He kissed her lightly on her cheek, ran his soft lips past her earlobe, and then buried his face into the crook of her neck.

A couple, passing by on the sidewalk, looked over at Harry and Rowena and smiled.

The warmth of his body intoxicated her. "Good-bye, Harry." She savored the moment before getting into the car.

He stood there as she started the engine and pulled away.

Down the block, she looked in her rearview mirror.

Harry was still standing there, looking after them.

Chapter Thirty-three

Daisy sat on the edge of the bed as Rowena finished packing. "I can't believe you and Mannie are leaving tomorrow."

"It seems surreal to me also. Actually this past year has been almost like a dream."

"I already can't wait for you to come back." The rims of Daisy's eyes filled up with tears.

"Now don't you go crying or you'll have me blubbering like a baby. I promise I'll stay in touch with e-mail."

"You better or I'll have to buy a plane ticket to come over to the States and personally scold you."

Rowena paused for a moment, holding a folded shirt in midair. "You know—I feel it in my bones that someday Mannie and I are going to live here in Cornwall." She put the garment in her suitcase.

Daisy perked up. "Do you really think so? What about Mannie's dad, won't he protest, I mean, who wouldn't fall in love with Mannie, yes?"

"If I had to guess, I'd say in the beginning he'll be attentive. But he once told me after we were married that he didn't want any kids. Heck, he wouldn't even allow me to have a pet. To tell you the truth, I don't think he likes children that much." Rowena stopped packing and sat on the edge of the bed.

"Well," she sighed. "No matter what the outcome, I hope only the best for both of you."

"Thank you for saying that, Daisy, You're a precious friend."

"Simon told me about Harry's ridiculous plan to move on someplace else. I hope he talked some sense into him." Daisy shook her head.

Rowena looked up at Daisy and her mind drifted to Aunt Maude, a woman who was instrumental in changing her life forever. Maude's gift has given her a place she longed to call home, memories and friends she'll never forget.

"Speaking of Simon, he'll be gone for the night and is coming back in the morning. He has some business concerning his new job starting up again." Daisy got up to leave the room. At the doorway she turned around. "Get a good night's sleep, girlfriend. See you at breakfast. We should get an early start, about eight o'clock to get you at Heathrow airport."

Rowena got under the covers and set her alarm for six o'clock.

The next morning, Daisy lightly rapped on Rowena's door and then entered. "Jesse has breakfast ready in the dining area. Simon just texted me, he'll be home shortly."

Rowena checked on her bundle of joy. *Such a sweet face.* "Look, she's grinning at something."

Daisy peeked at the baby. "Yes, she's dreaming about staying here forever, and plotting to convince you."

The girls giggled and turned on the monitor before they went downstairs.

"Jesse thanks so much for the wonderful breakfast. I should help you clean up, but I must be getting ready." As she stood up, Crookie, brushed up against Rowena's leg and she leaned to pet his soft coat. "Good morning, kitty, kitty."

"No worries, love. I'll get things in order quickly and we'll help you pack your things." Jesse started to clear the table.

Simon came in with Brengi on his heels. "I'm back." He looked around and grabbed a plate and gathered some food before Jesse put things away.

"Did the dog drag you in? Simon, you look tired." Rowena grinned.

"I'm fine, just didn't get a lot of sleep."

"I was beginning to wonder if you'd be back in time." Daisy looked relieved.

As Simon finished up, Rowena lifted her bag and stroller from the chair next to him. He tossed his napkin on his empty plate and got up. "I've got these." He took her belongings to the van.

Rowena went over to where Brengi was lying on a rug near the unlit fireplace. She sat down and petted him. "Good-bye 'ol boy, I promise to visit next year. I know you'll take good care of everybody."

He looked up at her with his puppy eyes, and a slight guttural sound came from his throat. It was as if he said, "I understand you."

Simon and Daisy sat in the front of the van while Rowena and Mannie sat in the back. As they backed out of the driveway, Jesse and Curtis stood at the door waving.

They turned down the lane and headed for the motorway.

"So, how does it feel to be going back to the States?" Simon asked as he drove.

"To tell you the truth, I'm anxious to see my family. Jesse allowed me to use her land line last evening to call them and I actually broke the news about Mannie."

"You did? What'd they have to say about that?" Daisy turned all the way around in her seat.

"Oh—my aunt's crazy happy, and with her I mean that literally." Rowena laughed. "Grandpa and Uncle Robert are excited too. As you know, I didn't even realize I was pregnant until after I arrived in England. I'm sure they'll give me a hard time for not telling them sooner.

"Yes, with everything going on in your life, you just thought your tummy upset was anxiety."

Rowena looked at her healthy baby and reflected on her misjudgment. "I appreciate how you understand."

Simon put on the radio and found a channel playing soft music. As the melodies filled the air, Rowena became wistful and rested her head back, closing her eyes. Her mind drifted to Harry, remembering the sensation of him softly kissing her neck, his wonderful scent.

The music stopped with the announcement of breaking news:

"Thirty miles east of Morcant, another woman was attacked last night. The victim fought off the assailant and he escaped. She was able to describe the man to police. No names or further information will be released at this time. Stay tuned—"

Simon turned down the radio. "I hope they find the rotten bugger."

Daisy and Rowena shared a frightened glance.

At the airport they checked in Rowena and Mannie's luggage.

Simon and Daisy accompanied them as far as the lounge next to the security line.

"Before you leave I have something to say to you." Simon put his hands in his jean pockets. "I hope you know Harry fancies you and the only reason he thought of leaving is because he can't stand the thought of losing you."

"Really? He said that?"

"In so many words he did. He told me, you're leery of him, but I have to tell you, Harry's a good bloke."

"Thank you, Simon. I believe you."

"Are you sure you and little Mannie will be alright?" Daisy said in Rowena's ear as she hugged her.

"We'll be fine." Rowena hugged her friend, almost afraid to let go, as her life would change for her once more.

"If anyone would love your child as his own, it would be Harry." Daisy whispered again, and then released her embrace from Rowena. She leaned down to Mannie in her stroller and kissed her on the cheek. "Good bye sweetie, Aunt Daisy loves you to the moon and back."

Rowena went over and put her arms around Simon. "Thank you, for everything."

"The pleasure's been mine." The typically stoic man gave her a robust hug. "It looks like you have everything in order, so I think we'll move on and leave you to it."

"Yes, you two get back to Morcant. There's plenty of time; Mannie and I'll just sit here and get our stuff organized. Thanks again. I love you both."

"We love you too." Daisy blew a kiss and she and Simon turned and walked away.

As Rowena sat in the chair close to the security line, out of the corner of her eye, she noticed someone approaching her. Eyeing the floor, a man in tasseled loafers stood before her. She looked up.

It was Hunter. He appeared different, drugged, and unkempt. As his mouth parted, it revealed strings of white sticky saliva. "Hello Rowena, fancy meeting you here," He failed to smile and his eyes pierced her with a murky green dullness.

"Hello Hunter. Are you traveling back to the States?"

"Not yet." His raked his teeth across his bottom lip and then licked them. The bluntness of his voice alarmed Rowena.

Uneasy, Rowena stood up and took Mannie out of her umbrella stroller and put her bag over her shoulder. She closed up the light weight carrier and with the baby in her arms, said to Hunter, "Good day." She scurried towards Security.

Rowena stepped into the rope barriers behind an older couple with a teenage girl. With a long line in front of her, the young girl turned around and looked at Mannie. "Aww, such a cute little baby. How old is she?"

With a false, uneasy smile Rowena answered the girl. "Five weeks."

The girl smiled back and looked into Mannie's face. The older woman spoke to the girl. "Sophie dear, here's your ticket." Sophie turned towards her grandmother and took her voucher.

From behind, Hunter brought his face to Rowena's ear. Her heart quickened and she froze. The heat and smell of his rancid breath on her neck sent shivers down her spine. "Don't move Rowena," he whispered in her ear. "I have a knife right at your kidney. You're not going through any scanners today."

Rowena felt the pointed pressure to her back.

"Did you think you just happened to see me here in England, Rowena? Your daft ex-husband hired me to have you followed. I didn't even know who I was stalking until you brought it to my attention. You're not too sexy puking your guts up, but, oh— that hug you gave me that day…I've killed two women waiting for you, but it didn't quite quench my thirst. I've been thinking about you, you sweet thing. Now— nice and easy, step out of line."

Rowena didn't move a muscle, not as much as a blink, she watched.

Had my gullible mind been at such a dark place 12 years ago I'd have put my life into the hands of a monster? Could I've allowed William to drive me to that madness? And now, this twisted beast prowled the streets at night, terrorizing the lovely village of Morcant?

Sophie turned around again and cooed at Mannie, touching the tip of her little nose with her finger. A couple of more people stepped into the roped area.

Hunter put more pressure onto the knife, penetrating her clothing.

She felt the prick of the knife entering just under her skin. She didn't wince. With only her eyes she glanced at the handle of the folded up umbrella stroller hooked on her forearm.

"Rowena!" A man shouted.

Harry's voice?

Rowena's grandfather had taught her vigilance when in danger.

NO MORE!—

In a split second, she thrust her baby into the teenager's arms.

Still standing with her back to Hunter, she lifted her leg and with every ounce of strength she had rammed her pointed boot heel down on Hunter's foot. She brought the same heel up and back-kicked him between his legs. The sound of steel hit the floor. In a flash, she swung around and positioned the stroller like a bat over her shoulder and slammed the wheels into the side of Hunter's head.

That's for Patty and Kara, you son-of-a-bitch!

Each breath Rowena took in and out were adrenaline ridden.

The people behind Hunter cowered back.

Hunter staggered and then looked up at Rowena, moaning.

Rowena doubled up her fist and with a force foreign to her, busted him just above his right eye, her ring boring into flesh.

And that's from me!

Screams echoed from the airport walls. Sophie stood back with her eyes wide open and hugged Mannie close to her. Her grandfather surrounded his arms around both of them and pulled them away.

Security grabbed Rowena— jerked her arms behind her back and handcuffed her.

"Harry! He's the killer!"

But Hunter shook his head and cleared the blood from his eyes—then ran past Harry.

Harry chased Hunter, caught the back of his shirt, and then encircled his arms under his armpits, locking both hands at his neck. He body slammed Hunter to the ground, his head hitting the floor. Harry pulled Hunter up by the hair and dropped his face on his knee, holding his skull until Security came.

Rowena went into a room with Officer Angie at the Police Station in the terminal at the airport. She closed the door. "You can take your shirt off now."

Rowena slipped off her top and felt the wet blood slide up her back.

When Officer Angie saw the wound, she winced, "Oh dear, we'd better call a doctor."

"Actually— could you please—umm, just bring in Harry, he's a physician."

Officer Angie looked up at Rowena. "I think we can do that." She went to summon him.

Harry appeared in the room, holding Mannie. He gave her to the officer and went to wash his hands. Angie held out a box of latex gloves and first aid kit.

As he applied some antiseptic, Rowena winced.

"Thank goodness, it's only a flesh wound." Harry let out a sigh. He dressed the cut and then he and Mannie left the room.

"Here, you can have this." Officer Angie handed Rowena a London Metropolitan Police XL t-shirt. "I'm going to have to keep your other shirt for evidence."

Rowena pulled the top over her head and put it on.

"I'm sorry to say you're going to have to stick around for a couple of days. We'll set you up at a hotel close to Metropolitan Central."

"Thanks, officer."

Officer Angie put her hand on Rowena's shoulder. "You've been through a lot today."

As Rowena walked out of the room in her oversized t-shirt, she met Harry and Mannie on a bench outside the office. He held the baby close to his chest, the side of his face resting on top of her head. When he looked up, beads of sweat dampened his pale forehead and his flushed cheeks shown bright under the florescent lights. "Mannie has a little heart shaped face, just like yours, even a little dimple on her chin."

Rowena sat down next to them. "Harry, you don't look well."

He peered up at her. His voice was choked. "I could have lost you—if that knife would have penetrated past the skin…."

As she stood in front of him, Rowena put both of her hands on each side of Harry's face and brought his chin up to gaze into his eyes. She lightly kissed one side of his mouth, and then the other, moving her lips to give little pecks all over his cheeks. "There. A million baby kisses. Does that make you feel any better?"

Harry smiled all the way up to his brown eyes. "It's a start." He winked.

Rowena sat down next to him and laid her head on his shoulder. "If you want me to tell you the truth, my hand hurts worse than my back." She shook her long slim fingers back and forth.

"Actually—you did show some pretty amazing maneuvers." Harry laid Mannie in her stroller. "Let me take a look." He gently took a hold of her throbbing hand. "Does that hurt?" He pressed the top and palm.

"Ouch, yes, a little bit."

"Wiggle your fingers."

She moved all of her digits.

"Nothing seems broken." He laid her hand on his thigh.

"Well." She lightly swirled her index finger on his upper leg. "Being raised by a grandpa who was a boxing champ did have its perks."

"Your grandpa was a prizefighting title holder? Hmm—you don't say. I like the guy already."

Rowena lifted her head and looked squarely at Harry. "I can't believe it. Those are the exact words Mr. McGreevy said about my grandpa."

Officer Angie came to where they were sitting. "I have some information about your assailant. His real name is Janus Hinckley.

He runs his own detective agency, his specialty is finding cheating or missing spouses. We've run his prints and his bio and discovered links to other murders. The souls of his shoes matchup with evidence also."

"Like a serial killer?' Rowena drew in a breath and put her back against the wall.

"Wait—nothing has been confirmed. But breaking into vacant homes to set up a temporary residence makes him a suspect in other cases."

Rowena thought about that night long ago when she went back to Mapletown to try and find him. "So he moves all around. That would make it difficult to track him down."

"We hope further investigation will prove our suspicions." Officer Angie put both of her thumbs up. "Why don't the two of you take the baby and go get a bite to eat. It's on us." She handed a food voucher to Rowena." The police woman then turned around and walked back towards to the station.

"Thank you." Rowena called out down the hall.

Harry and Rowena strolled with Mannie into The Three Bells restaurant and found a quiet table in the corner of the softly lit room.

"I'll just have your Caesar Salad, please," Rowena said to the waiter.

"I'll take the Superfood Salad. And a side plate of brioche baps, please." Harry handed back their menus. "Would you like any wine, Rowena?"

"White wine, please." Rowena gathered up her hair and placed it to one side of her shoulder.

Harry became silent for a moment. "I've been meaning to apologize for how rude I was to you that night in regards to your question about Kara."

"Apologize for what? You don't have anything to be sorry for. I was completely out of line in asking. It wasn't and will never be any of my business."

"No—you asked a fair request. So, I'm telling you now. Yes—I did care about Kara and I had a bit of relationship going with her, as discreet as it was. Honestly, nothing too terribly serious. Still, I've been quite saddened by it all."

"I'm so sorry."

"Kara knew that day in the restaurant when you came in and we shared lunch, I'd fallen for you and it was over between us."

"Please tell me that in the end, she was alright with things."

"I hope so... she was a troubled woman."

Rowena reached over and put her hand on Harry's.

Harry paused for a moment, his leg gently brushed Rowena's under the table. "Let's just promise from here on out, we'll always be open and honest with each other."

"Of course."

The waiter brought the food and poured the white wine into crystal goblets.

Harry's paleness became replaced with a confident glow about him. He sampled the white liquid and nodded to the server.

"Thank you, these buns smell wonderful," Rowena inhaled the hot steaming bread as she took off the cloth napkin covering them.

"Very good, enjoy." The young man hurried along to another table.

In the carrier, Mannie fell asleep to the soft background music.

Rowena put some butter on her roll and took a nibble. A bit of the melted topping dripped from the corner of her mouth. She nabbed it lightly with her finger. "So, besides being my distraction, tackling a serial killer, and patching up your girlfriend, what else did you do today?"

"Are you my girlfriend, Rowena?" He took a bite from a cherry tomato and blinked his eyes.

"I don't know." She pressed her lips together and tried not to smile. "Does Mannie get a promissory teething ring?"

"If that would make her mummy happy, Mannie can have one with a gold handle."

Rowena took a sip of her wine and with the goblet still to her lips, lingered her gaze at Harry's eyes.

"I'm sure the police provided you with meager lodging accommodations." He circled his finger around the top of his wine glass. "How about a little upgrade?" He raised his eyebrows.

"Only if you stay with me." Rowena took a small bite of her salad and slowly pulled the fork from her lips.

"Oh, I'm not going anywhere." He grinned, his dimple appearing. "I've a physician friend already coming to my surgery for the next couple of day, yes. I'll book a room at the Egerton House Hotel."

"It's just dawned on me; I don't even have a toothbrush. Oh—and my coat…the police kept that for evidence also." Rowena laughed.

"We'll get you something to clean your teeth… and I'll buy you the sexist coat in London.

"A warm one will do fine." She playfully eyed him sideways.

"Would you settle for warm and sexy, yes?" He slyly smiled back and took another sip of his wine.

"Oh—Harry, something else just occurred to me. I want to give my Auntie Maude a toast." Rowena picked up her goblet and clicked it with Harry's. "Thank you, my precious aunt. Thank you, just thank you…for everything."

"Well…Doc Hollister." Harry began. "Thanks a lot… For neglecting to tell me what a beautiful niece you have." He winked at Rowena and then got serious. "To Maude, my dear friend, you were a person of indisputable probity. And the kindest woman I've ever had the honor of knowing."

Rowena paused for a second, taken in by Harry's polished words, and then asked, "So, you'll really be here with me the next couple of days? I'd like you to be."

"Of course, I'll always be there for you. Always." Harry stopped for a second before he spoke again. "I'd swim the Atlantic; I'd climb every mountain in America if it brings me to you."

"You know, you did that already for me today. If you hadn't arrived just when you did—well, let's just say, you're my hero. You have a way about you, Harry."

"I came to the airport today with the express purpose of stopping you from leaving England or I should say, I couldn't bear the thought of you being gone from my life."

A soft yet potent sentiment resounded vociferously in Rowena's mind. She could still hear her Aunt Agnes's words from that one pathetic Thanksgiving Day 12 years ago.

A man will walk a thousand miles barefoot on a path with broken glass and swim the length of the Mississippi River with only a snorkel and a wind breaker, if he really loves you.

Harry took both of Rowena's hands and brought them to his mouth, closing his eyes. "I love you Rowena. I knew the moment I first met you, you'd be in my life—and besides, who else will be there to patch up all the cuts and nicks you seem to so readily acquire?"

They both laughed.

Love does not consist in gazing at each other,
But in looking outward together in the same direction.
(Antoine de Saint-Exupery)

About the Author

LeAnn L. Morgan has written three award-winning short stories: Thomasine's Journal-A Midwest Gothic Tale, Even a Beautiful Swan, and A Writer Takes Her Pen to Write the Words Again. Morwen Cottage is her debut novel. She lives in Galesburg, Illinois.

CPSIA information can be obtained
at www.ICGtesting.com
Printed in the USA
BVHW030934100419
544546BV00017B/26/P